Wreckful's Run

Itamar Bernstein

GB

WRECKFUL'S RUN

GB (December 2011)

ISBN-13 9781468083071

WRECKFUL'S RUN

PART ONE

A Clash of Civilizations

The light that emanated from the twelve stained glass windows bathed the Synagogue at the Hadassah University Medical Center in Ein Kerem, Jerusalem in brilliant glow. The young man illuminated by the sun filtered through the vivid colors seemed to float in the glare, transformed in time and space. He was reading the placard by Marc Chagall.

"This is my modest gift to the Jewish people who have always dreamt of biblical love, friendship and of peace among all peoples. This is my gift to that people who lived here thousands of years ago among the other Semitic peoples."

The young man ambled on the Jerusalem stone floor into the square forming the window's pedestal, and lifted his radiant face to gaze up at the Jewish imagery, his lips moving, silently repeating the various quotations of the Biblical blessings on the twelve tribes of Israel. He then left the Synagogue to the hospital proper, smiling.

*

Inspector Michael Inbar of the Jerusalem police arrived at Hadassah less than two hours later, and went to speak with the hospital receptionist, a middle aged woman. "Tell me about that man," he inquired softly.

"Mesmerizing presence," she said, bewildered.

"Age?"

"About 30. I'd say. "

"Height?"

"I don't know. Not very tall. "

"Hair, eye color, body build?"

"I don't remember. He asked for Ariel Sharon's room. I told him it's at the 7th floor, He said 'thanks' and went to the elevator."

"You just showed him to Prime Minister Sharon's room, without alerting anyone? Weren't you instructed otherwise?"

"I was. But I forgot all about it. He dazed me."

"Just like that? Juices flowing to drop your duties at the sight of young men?"

"It wasn't like that at all. More like he cast some spell over me."

6

On which note Inbar waived a hand in tired frustration, proceeded lethargically to the elevator, and rode it to the 7th floor.

*

Inbar exited to a long corridor, enhanced by wall paintings of museum league. In the misty haze of the cloudy midday filtered through high art stained glass windows on both ends of the corridor, he saw four security guards standing by a heavy looking door of one room, and walked the otherwise vacant space to them. Producing his Jerusalem police ID, he gave gradually awakening ears to a puzzling account of the psychedelic kind.

"He exited the elevator and crossed the length of the empty corridor toward us," recounted one of the guards of the two who sat by the room in the morning, having described the subject of their bewilderment in the same paucity of detail as the hospital receptionist. "I watched him transfixed with a very pleasant feeling. He said 'I come in peace and good intentions' and went inside this Sharon room."

Inbar inspected the special security steel door of the room. "Seems pretty much impregnable, welded steel construction, tamper resistant features and all. I see no signs of forced entry. Wasn't the door locked?" he asked incredulously.

"It must have been," made the incipient guard. "It definitely was," affirmed the second guard. "I happened to check it locked just before he came from the elevator. "

"How did he enter then?"

"Beats me. He laid his right hand lightly on the round door lock, rotated it clockwise, pushed the door in, entered the room and closed the door behind him."

"And you just stayed put, both of you? I reckon Shin Bet now sends junkies to guard the former Prime Minister of Israel. And next he disappeared from Sharon's room into thin air, right?"

"No. The door opened, he came out, smiled to us and returned the way of the elevator. "

"How long was he inside the room while you were absently high on your mushrooms, or whatever clouded your brains?"

"I don't remember," the guards answered simultaneously." I wasn't lucid, but I haven't taken any drugs, alcohol or similar substance. Swear to God," one of them stated. The second nodded "Same here. It was like I was hypnotized."

"Unlock the door, fruitcakes," bellowed Inbar. "I'll measure the flow of your hallucinations."

*

Inbar looked at Ariel Sharon lying dead to the world in his standard hospital bed. Memories of his wife Rona in the same situation, many years earlier, reared in Inbar's mind. "*Sic transit gloria mundy*," she'd certainly proclaim in Latin at the sorry sight of Ariel Sharon here. Worldly things are fleeting indeed. The great winner, nicknamed "bulldozer," had been comatose since January 2006, following a severe stroke. His doctors pronounced him in a permanent vegetative state.

Who'll wake him from this slumber, to lead his people in confident security once again? Miracles that had benefitted Rona rarely happen in the dark confines of life and death.

At that point Sharon opened his eyes and gazed at Inbar. The eyes then moved sideways. Inbar followed to watch the TV screen fixed on the far wall. It flickered a ceremony broadcast around the world from the United

States. Sharon then opened his mouth and with a clear voice, his words throbbing around Inbar, acknowledged "Forty fifth President inaugurated? I must have been a sack of potatoes here a very long time."

2

The freighter Mimosa was cruising up the calm waters of the Bab el Mandeb strait in the pre-dawn of a mid winter weekday. The ship, carrying a Liberian flag, had set sail from Yemen and took a day to reach the somewhat narrow entrance that connects the Gulf of Aden to the Red Sea. The ship's pilot standing aft in the waning moonlight heard a familiar sound, scanned the clatter's direction and spotted the helicopter generating it flying low toward him, then climbing some to hover directly overhead. A different chainsaw sound coming from the sea below called the pilot's attention to several speed boats packed with commandos. Within minutes the sounds subsided into rumbling and the boats coasted the freighter. Ladders that appeared from them were laid against the freighter's starboard side, and the soldiers scrambled and scaled them to the deck.

Before the pilot could sound an alarm on deck, he heard the helicopter's loudspeaker warning in English that a capture operation had begun, telling the crew members to lay down on the floor. The pilot conformed and lay face down on the cold metallic surface, his eyes following several of the soldiers entering the bridge, in the dawn's early light. Soft breeze carrying the fragrance of salt over water caressed his face as the ship entered the wider waters of the Red Sea, heading due North.

*

"We've shadowed the Mimosa since its departure from the port of Aden, in Yemen," the CIA Director informed the President and national security officials in their meeting early next week at the White House. "Its shipment was wiggled. Within a few days it was loaded from one freighter to another in different ports. On an Iranian boat at the Iranian port of Bandar Abas, to a Panamanian ship at the Jebel Ali port in the United Arab Emirates, and then a third time in Aden onto the Mimosa that our special forces seized."

"Any other evidence of Iranian connection for the intercepted ship?" inquired the President.

"We have reliable intelligence that it's ultimately held by the Iranian state shipping company IRISI, which conceals ultimate ownership of its fleet under several non-Iranian flags of convenience, constantly changes names of its ships, and other subterfuges."

"Where is it now?"

"Docked in Jeddah, Saudi Arabia, where we've thoroughly searched it, having first sorted all cargo containers on the quay."

"Can we trust the Saudis' security on this?"

"The Saudis are religious extremists also, but downright realistic and pragmatic. They believe that Iran seeks to reduce them to subservient state. They are extremely apprehensive of Iran, ever since Iranian Shi'a extremists back in 1979 seized the great mosque in Mecca, taking hundreds of pilgrims hostage and calling for the overthrow of the Saudi monarchy. The Saudis crushed them and beheaded many of the captured militants. A similar episode nevertheless happened again in 1981. At which time the Iranian rebels tried to take Mecca itself."

"Is that where you found the middle range missile with that primitive nuclear device, now hopefully safely here in the US?"

"Yes. Hidden behind bags of polyethylene."

"Where was that ship going to?"

"Galveston, Texas."

"Can we monitor all Iranian ship movements in the commercial shipping routes along our East Coast?"

"Iran may use ships with radar and technical equipment similar to the scores of surrounding vessels. Investigating which ship has a launching pad would take months," the Homeland Security Secretary said. "And this would be even farther complicated by a possible deployment by a terrorist organization supplied by Iran, rather than Iran directly."

"They certainly would take every step to conceal their involvement in an attack on us from a cargo ship," stated the President.

"They do like to keep their fingerprints off in terror circumstances. A committee that studied this scenario warned that we may never be able to find out who was ultimately responsible for an attack. To erase all traces, the Iranians could simply have the ship sunk."

"Do they possess the technology for a precision hit on a target in the US?"

"They routinely brag they do," informed the CIA Director. "As one of their generals stated to their news agency during our previous Administration, for whatever such statement is worth, 'Iran is now one of the countries that possess the technology to fire missiles from ships with maximum precision and minimum deviation.' Be that as it may, they don't really need precision for the scarier scenario."

"Which is?"

"Iran could fairly easily use a regular cargo ship, if it's close enough to our shores, as a launch platform to send a limited range missile armed with a small primitive nuclear device to explode some 70 miles above the center of the United States. The explosion would not be intended to cause direct damage, but by the intense burst of energy to form a radiation wave, called Electro Magnetic Pulse, or EMP, causing all electronics over a massive area, possibly the entire continental US, to shut down immediately. "

"That would flash us back to the 19th century."

"Everything would fall silent. Communications, transport, electricity, infrastructure. Nothing would work, from lighting to computers to elevators. This would thoroughly devastate civilian life. It would also kill many, not least because water pumps and filters would stop working, spoiling and cutting supply. It would also cause an estimated 1-2 trillion dollars in damages and take four to ten years to recover."

"I'm sure there are less alarming expert opinions, but we must act firmly on the worst case scenario." The President stated. "We can't take the risk that the national consequences of such EMP destroying our electrical grid would be far devastating, with long term country wide intolerable harm inflicted on our civilian population so dependent on our electricity hungry infrastructure." After a long pause, the President decided, "We won't let the fanatic Jihadist apocalyptic leaders of Iran detonate any nuclear device, rudimentary as it may be, over 'the great Satan'. And do so without attribution, for God's sake, we should take decisive action now. "

"Your operative instructions?" requested the Defense Secretary.

" Operation Strangejad is a go, ASAP."

"Thank you Madam President. With the former President, that would have been unthinkable."

"Thank all involved in this bloodless compliant boarding. We now face whales of hurdles to surmount."

3

The rain was torrential in Jerusalem on the next
morning when Michael Inbar descended from a city bus at
Zalman Shazar Boulevard, following the young man pictured
and videoed by many security cameras at Hadassah hospital,
including Sharon's room. The subject unhurriedly walked
to an underground pedestrian passageway. Inbar followed
under his umbrella, folding it upon entrance to the
passageway. He stopped casually, acting a cellular
conversation, as the subject was screened by the security
personnel before he entered the Central Bus Station building.
Inbar replaced the cellphone in his pocket and advanced for
the same security check. He didn't have a gun on him and
therefore was cleared quick enough to proceed after the
young man, through the second main level of the building.
Inbar stopped a moment, turning his face to a bakery outlet
when the subject paused before a video game parlor, gazing
into it. With his black hooded top sweatshirt he looked like
many of the hoodlums inside the parlor. He then proceeded
casually to the stairway, descending for the third level of
the station. Inbar followed, stopping for a moment to look

at the game parlor's showcase, pleasurably noticing a World of Warcraft game cover, marketing a "Reckful Special Edition" in bold red, large print. Inbar then resumed following the young man, subject of his instant attention, down the stairs to the station's departure hall.

That subject stopped to check a large digital display board that posted upcoming departure time, then proceeded to wait by the door marked "4." Inbar stopped some distance away, before the door marked "1." Presently a bus marked 444: Jerusalem CBS - Ein Gedi - Ein Bokek - Eilat CBS (Express) pulled into its slot at the departure platform. The young man entered through the number 4 door and boarded that bus, followed by the other passengers, Inbar among them.

*

The bus was going down the spectacular road eastward from Jerusalem to Jericho, it would make it from its start around 800 meters above sea level to its end at 300 odd meters below sea level, a distance of about 40 kilometers, in about 45 minutes.

From Jerusalem's Mount of Olives, the road winds downward toward *Jerusalem's Shayyah* neighborhood, where they came in view of the entire Judean hills wilderness, and the deep rift valley of the Jordan river. While other passengers surely enjoyed the view, Inbar was ruminating about his severe accident many years before on the narrow, steep, rough and barren road, winding by imposing limestone cliffs below.

When they passed Jericho, the young man stood up, walked over to the bus driver and quietly said something to him. Amazingly, the bus driver then made an unscheduled stop, and asked all passengers to descend from the bus. For some reason, they all complied.

The rain had stopped as they came out of the bus, and now the colors of the desert were rapidly turning rosier every minute with the sun emerging between the clouds. The pure light desert breeze was playing with the young man's hair as he climbed a hill overlooking the river Jordan. Inbar was looking at the sun swept desert rolling south to the Dead Sea when he heard a clear, transcending voice and turned around.

The young man then solemnly proclaimed: "Here Joshua, son of Nun, performed a miracle like Moses before him did at the Red Sea. God caused the waters of the Jordan to pile themselves upstream in a heap for Joshua son of Nun. The river bed was left dry for the feet of the tribes of Israel. Now we are gathered in the vicinity of the place where God made a sure sign of His intentions toward Israel, and of His confirmation of Joshua's role as Moses' successor. In this area my brothers have lived to renew their vows before God, to fit them for their glorious mission and salvation in His Kingdom. But you need no longer wait for

19

another like Joshua to lead you to the promised land of God's era."

As he finished speaking, a wall of cloud came from behind and overshadowed the passengers and they reboarded the bus. It continued south along the western shore of the Dead Sea. The young man descended at the first of four Ein Gedi stops, some 45 kilometers from Jericho. Inbar followed with several other passengers. The bleached wilderness below the steep limestone cliffs greeted them in compelling silence with a heavy smell of sulphur and dank hostility.

*

There were several trails from the ticket office to the Ein Gedi site. The young man took one of them seemingly without looking at the signs. Inbar followed in some distance, turning down by a sign indicating "Tel Goren" and "Synagogue," acutely aware of the flash flood that could be caused here by the continuing rain. The subject was walking steadily, unhurriedly and confidently on the trail, winding through tall pines and palm trees, Inbar proceeding in his steps under an umbrella, between silts of rock formation, under canopies of papyrus reeds. He knew the trail leads to Ein Gedi's Byzantine era synagogue.

The young man went through a group of small dwellings, surrounding the synagogue, pausing a moment to look at two ritual baths and entered the trapezoid shaped structure, now covered by a white tent. Inbar stopped by a palm tree short of the tent, the cell phone in his left hand shooting in video mode while he observed the subject crossing the central prayer hall, by the square of stumps that supported the roof, to the mosaic floor. He stood there a moment, then stepped to the left rectangular section, where he stood a few seconds, his back turned to Michael. Next he moved to a long aisle, stood there contemplatively for several moments. He then turned back, against the wind. Whirlwinds of water surrounded him and dripped under his chin as he exited the tent and advanced directly toward Inbar, smiled and greeted "Good morning, Michael." Inbar responded with a smile, holding tight to his umbrella. Before he could say anything the young man was gone in the swelling gusts of wind and the loud blast of falling hail.

Inbar entered the synagogue, folded his umbrella and went to the mosaic floor, now using the cell phone to take several photos of it, concentrating on its central circle design of peacock chicks and adult birds. He walked the black paving to the left rectangular section. It only had a basin for washing hands. He shot that, as well as the dedication mosaic by the long aisle. He felt cold and wet and was happy to return to the bus back to the comforting relative warmth of his office in Jerusalem.

4

The diminutive, feisty President of Iran, full of himself and always in need to prove his endowment to his nation and the world, was directly broadcasting a speech on Iranian state television, at Sahand TV main building in Tabriz, a city he came to visit after an earthquake two days earlier. As always, he started the speech by reverently blessing the 12th Imam, whose return will soon be hastened, he declaimed the usual earthquake consolation, following with death threats against the 'great Satan' America, and the 'little Satan', the 'Zionist entity', ominously citing the infamous Hadith that postulates the Day of Judgment won't come unless the Jews are pulled out from hiding behind rocks and trees and killed.

Having finished the speech, the President under heavy security guard descended to the basement parking of the building, where he was ushered to the back seat of one of seven identical looking black Mercedes limousines. His motorcade then exited to the surface streets, about three miles from the center of Tabriz. A US spy satellite immediately zoomed on it at coordinates 38°3'34"N 46°19'56"E, adjusted to monitor its progression southbound to Tabriz International Airport, at 38° 8' 2" North, 46° 14' 5" East. A Predator drone that took off earlier from a NATO airbase in nearby Azerbaijan was now approaching the limousine column in full view of the snow covered dormant volcano mountain range of Sahand.

A few minutes later, the motorcade advancing slowly on a mountain road snaking in surrounding high altitude flora, a wild boar with dark dense bristles suddenly emerged from the trees lining the roadside ahead. A shot crackled from the dense vegetation and stopped the animal cold. It fell and lay on the middle of the southbound lane.

At an air force base in the US, a pilot sitting in a leather captain's chair at the controls of the drone watched the motorcade stopping, half a world away. He angled his joystick and the drone turned toward it, while the pilot powered up two Hellfire missiles under its wings. At that point a crew member operating the drone's cameras videoed tiny white flashes that appeared by the first and third limousines in the column.

Two Iranian policemen rode their motorcycles from the procession, close to the immobilized wild pig, then continued ahead and stood down to hold traffic on the northbound lane. The drone was now circling high overhead.

At an Air National Guard base in Terre Haute, Ind., an Air Force analyst whose job was to monitor the video to advise which limousine carried the Iranian President watched the incident unfold on the drones feed. The analyst, a technical sergeant, was messaging a minute by minute report to the mission's intelligence coordinator at March Air reserve base in California.

24

The analyst observed that the flashes, heat signature of gunfire, were firing at the direction of the trees on the right side of the road, from the first and third limousines in the column. Twelve seconds later he typed "Iranian President inside second limousine, " sending that report to the mission intelligence coordinator, who then passed it to the crew controlling the drone.

"Kill the target," the CIA official standing behind the pilot ordered.

"Roger," complied the pilot, pushing a button on his joystick. In fifteen seconds, the Iranian President would be dead.

*

At the same time the drone was circling above the President's motorcade, the chauffeur of a Grand Ayatollah Shi'a Twelver was negotiating the traffic in Qom, Iran. He was a bit late to the notorious religious seminary of that holy city, where the influential hard line cleric was scheduled to give an important lecture. He was driving on a busy thoroughfare, on the right of two Eastbound lanes, following a white Toyota van that had advanced before his limo from a side street several blocks back. The van came to a stop at the next intersection's red light and the limo stopped behind it. The chauffeur didn't pay attention to a small Japanese car that moved slowly from the left to the right lane, and stopped behind him. He was making an embarrassed cellphone call to an administrator at the seminary, advising that the lecturer might be a little late. The complaint implied in the administrator's reply that "hundreds of students are waiting" didn't do much to calm the edgy caller.

Two minutes later, the light changed to green, but the white van remained stopped. The chauffeur honked in frustration to no avail. He wanted to pass around the van, but couldn't change to the left lane, though it was free now, the little sedan behind him blocking the maneuver. He came out of the limo advancing angrily toward the driver door of the van. But when he reached its side by the left rear wheel, the backdoors of the van suddenly opened. Two masked men holding submachine guns sprayed the limo with bullets, hitting the Grand Ayatollah in the back seat. The backdoors then closed in the van, which proceeded to cross the intersection eastbound. A woman then exited the small Japanese car, pistol in hand. She walked over to the limo, opened the right back door and verified the killing with a shot to the holy man's head. She then returned to the small sedan and drove it past the limo to the left lane, continuing forward across the intersection. The intersection's light was still green when the two vehicles disappeared into a side street branching westbound from the thoroughfare.

*

Sometime later on that day in Istanbul, Turkey, a top class Iranian jurist, foremost member of the powerful Guardian Council, entered the lobby of the Hilton hotel located on the city's European side that he'd checked into a day earlier. He walked the hall to the restaurant at the East side of the hotel, noticing a long legged young woman sitting by a table on the terrace facing the Asian side. He stepped outside to the terrace, sat at a table next to hers and asked a waiter for a glass of juice.

"Don't you prefer wine?" she flirted as the waiter brought his juice.

"I don't drink alcohol, and it shouldn't be served at a hotel here," he correctly muttered.

"Too flat for me. Are you here by yourself?" she made, opening a pack of Kents and gazing directly into his eyes while holding a cigarette in her right hand.

"No. You?" He answered.

"Not any more."

27

He moved over to her table, placing his juice on it, then standing over her, lighting her cigarette, not oblivious to her generous cleavage, and sat at the seat across from her.

"Cigarette?" She asked, bending forward a bit extending a cigarette over the table in her left hand.

"Not now," he muttered, still glancing at her full bosom.

"You here for business?" she enquired, replacing the rejected Kent in the package.

"I came for a conference," now sipping of the juice. "What is it that you do?"

"I'm a journalist, traveling the world," still gazing directly into his eyes. "I'm going to my room now. Care to keep me company at my Guest Room Plus?" She extinguished her cigarette in the ashtray and put on a blue felt wide brimmed hat, slanting it forward. "I'm making myself sexy for you."

"Sure, but I don't have time to gaze at the sea view from your balcony… or mine. I'm leaving Istanbul this evening."

They had sex and he left on time, unaware of the ricin powder she'd managed to slip into his juice at the restaurant while he was distracted by her allure. He had difficulty breathing, sweating on the plane to Tehran, and a feeling of tightness in the chest after deplaning at Imam Khomeini International Airport. His skin turned blue by the time an ambulance took him, and he was dead on arrival at the hospital, never knowing that scores of other key hardcore principalist officials of the theocratic regime perished in various sinister ways on that same day.

5

"Good looking guy," remarked Rona.

"Everything is relative," Inbar contested morosely, his grieving mind still always unfavorably comparing every young man to his son Guy, many years after his death.

"I know this synagogue well," she said. "The white tent over it can even be seen from the main Dead Sea road. Who's this guy to you, Michael?"

They were standing by a computer in the living room of their Yemin Moshe apartment in Jerusalem watching the video Inbar had taken in Ein Gedi on the monitor.

Inbar nodded, "Just someone who's tingled my curiosity. Not much of a police matter. He's obviously pretty harmless, though he did inexplicably manage to enter Prime Minister Sharon's hospital room, without permission, some six weeks ago."

"Was that before Sharon woke up from his coma?"

"Yeah, couple hours before that. Just a coincidence. I watched the video taken of him by the security cameras. He did nothing but intensely gaze at Sharon, then walked out of the room."

"Run this synagogue video again, Michael. He seems to have been interested mainly by the mosaics."

"The central hall's mosaic carpet is certainly beautiful. It's decorated with a pattern of four-petalled flowers; in the center is a circle with four birds and on the corners of the outer, square frame are pairs of peacocks. The decoration opposite the beam included three seven-branched candelabra."

"Right Michael, I've seen that on my visit there a few years ago, after the site was renovated. It was found several years before, when a tractor hit a mosaic floor while preparing land for agricultural use. Excavations of the site revealed this synagogue that served the Ein Gedi Jewish community as of the third century, our era."

"Before we get to this mosaic, though, I've noticed a black swastika pattern in the center of the simple white floor. It's a tough connection, but he didn't pay attention to it."

"I believe this pattern has been interpreted as a decorative motif or as a good luck symbol, Michael."

"Makes sense. He doesn't strike me as a neo-Nazi. Going back to the mosaic, he must have been just admiring its art. Come to think of it, he lingered longer by the inscriptions on the floor of the western aisle."

"Right Michael. I can see that on the video now. He stood there several minutes, apparently reading them."

"I've also read two of them that are in Hebrew. One bears biblical names: Adam, Seth, Enosh, Kenan, Mehalalel, Jared, Enoch, Methuselah, Lamech, Noah, Shem, Ham and Japheth."

"The names of the thirteen fathers of the world according to Chronicles Chapter one."

"The other Hebrew inscription features names of the twelve signs of the zodiac and the twelve months of our Hebrew calendar; the three patriarchs: Abraham, Isaac and Jacob; and the names of the three companions of Daniel: Hananiah, Mishael and Azariah; and a blessing: Peace upon Israel. I couldn't read the other two inscriptions… they're in Aramaic. These are actually the ones where he stood longest, though."

"Right, the video shows that now. Can you zoom on his face?"

"Will do, love," Michael complied.

"Thanks… Can't see his expression that clearly from the fuzzy profile. You should have taken better than a cellphone camera. Anyway, I'd say he evinces pleasure. Enigmatic expression, won't you say?"

"Yeah, sort of a Mona Lisa smile," Michael exited the video application and displayed the pictures he'd taken of the subject Aramaic inscriptions on the monitor screen. Rona read the first inscription. "It mentions the local community as well as private donors who contributed toward the construction and maintenance of the synagogue."

"Notice anything unusual?"

"One inscription includes a warning and a curse. It reads

> *Warnings to those who commit sins causing dissension in the community, passing malicious information to the gentiles, or revealing the secrets of the town.*

> *The one whose eyes roam over the entire earth and sees what is concealed will uproot this person and his seed from under the sun and all the people will say, 'Amen. Selah'.*

"What do you make of that?"

" Seems like some magical incantation to me. Notice the command, that everybody must repeat the concluding 'Amen Selah.' This is the standard ending text of swearing talismans. The Amen Sela text usually appears many times on talismans, once after each oath."

"All about the 'secrets of the town.' What might that have been?"

"Beats me. Maybe something relating to the production methods of the prized Persimmon perfume, exclusive to the place, its vineyards celebrated from King Solomon's times, or some other economic secret of the area."

"Could it be related to some Jewish religious secret? Note the prohibition on 'passing malicious information to the gentiles'. If it were an economic secret it would prohibit revelation to everyone outside the community, Jewish as well as gentile."

"You mean like some Dead Sea Scrolls texts? They were authored in neighboring Qumran. But I'm afraid that's over my depth, or maybe I prefer sticking to romantics, such as 'my beloved is unto me as a cluster of campfire in the vineyards of Engedi' in the Song of Solomon. Why don't you ask Zalman Ganot, your *Deus Ex Machina* from the Israel Antiquities Authority."

At that note Michael composed an email to Ganot, as follows:

"What's the meaning of that ominous warning in the Aramaic inscription at the Ein Gedi synagogue?"

*

A few days later, at his office in the Jerusalem police headquarters, Michael received Ganot's response, which read tersely as always "check the names."

Inbar googled that. He reckoned the relevant text must be in the second Aramaic inscription, translated as followed:

"*May they be remembered for good: Yose and Ezron and Hizziqiyu the sons of Halfi. Anyone causing a controversy between a man and his friend, or whoever slanders his friend before the Gentiles, or whoever steals the property of his friend, or whoever reveals the secret of the town to the Gentiles—He Whose eyes range through the whole earth and Who sees hidden things, He will set His face on that man and on his seed and will uproot him from under the heavens. And all the people said: Amen and Amen Selah. Rabbi Yose the son of Halfi, Hiziqiyu the son of Halfi, may they be remembered for good,* "

At which point Inbar exclaimed "Damn his riddles," slamming his computer. His secretary knew better than leaving the safety of her workspace to inquire what happened at his office. She sighed, watching the spellbinding huge anti-government demonstrations in Tehran, broadcast nonstop on the TV screen mounted on a wall in the station's public waiting room, visible from her desk.

6

In the conference area aboard her global office of international security and diplomacy, 30,000 feet above Montana, the U.S. President seated in a leather chair heading the oval spotlessly polished wooden conference desk, the sealed device called "*The Football*" holding the codes for launching a nuclear attack by her left side, was receiving an intelligence briefing of the Iran situation from the CIA Director, seated in the side chair to her right. Four other security and military officials flanked both sides of the desk.

"Would the efforts we took be sufficient to destabilize the Mullahs, to a point where they would be effectively pressured to stop Iran's nuclear enrichment program and other terrorist plots against us?" inquired the President.

"Not unless they believe a crippling military operation against them is about to happen, I'm afraid."

"If so, our biggest priority now is overthrowing the Iranian theocratic regime," the President concluded. " Are we going to get that revolution anytime soon?"

"We're supporting anti-Iranian elements in the region as well as opposition groups within Iran. The demonstrations coming on the heels of the elimination of many hard line high officials genuinely reflect the deep anti-government sentiments of many Iranians. But Iranians in rural areas outside Tehran and some other big cities are firmly religious, and support the regime. We therefore believe toppling it from the inside isn't going to happen at this time."

"War is the only workable solution. Let's try to do it by proxy, before we put Americans in harms way. Can the Israelis manage that?"

"I believe so," the Air Force general opined from the second chair on the President's left.

"But that may trigger the firing of thousands of missiles at Israel from Lebanon and Gaza, by Iran's puppets Hezbollah and Hamas," said the Secretary of Defense.

"I don't believe so," estimated the CIA Director. "The Iranians respect and fear Sharon. He would certainly wipe the entire country off the map. They'd probably sit quiet, because they don't have nuclear tipped missiles yet."

"I'll talk to Sharon today," said the President. "Make sure our pilots in the area do not impair the Israelis, and adjust their rules of engagement accordingly."

An hour later, Air Force One landed without incident at Edwards Base Airport, California where the President deplaned to a sunny February day, followed by an assistant carrying the doomsday suitcase.

PART TWO

Wreckful

7

Colonel Avi "Wreckful" Inbar of the Israel Air force (IAF) was flying his F-16s "Sufa" 27,000 feet over Natanz in central Iran when he got contact of five Iranian Mig 29s coming at him from 10 o'clock at a distance of 13 miles. He knew in and out the capabilities of the very advanced Russian made aircraft, last in the Mig series, as three of those same planes were loaned to the IAF by a foreign country several years before. He had practiced innumerable dog fights against top IAF test pilots flying them. He knew that these first line combat aircraft in the world required precise, soft maneuvering to lock on for a kill.

Wreckful opened his afterburner and concentrated on his radar screen. It locked on the Migs and fed the information to the missiles beneath the F-16s wings. He cleared his formation to fire, pushed the launch button and watched two Sparrow missiles streak away toward the Migs, one from his aircraft and the second from number two flanking his right. But the Migs evaded the Sparrows, which flew harmlessly into cloudless blue sky of a February morning. As the distance closed very fast, Wreckful flew directly toward the lead Mig. It broke right, blinking first to avoid a head on collision, the maneuver exposing its hot tail pipes to Wreckful's heat seeking Python 5 missiles. Wreckful cranked 135 degrees to the left, to stay with the Mig, locked the Python on it, pushed the launch button and watched the all aspect missile streak to a perfect hit.

Wreckful turned hard right, sideways glancing the Iranian pilot ejecting from the Mig. He leveled the F-16, just when another Mig exploded higher to his right. He realized that his number two had downed that one. At that point number four shouted for Wreckful to take evasive action, as one of the Migs was now on his tail. He looked back and saw that one very close behind. He immediately pitched his nose up to let the Mig pass below him, then rolled over the top, descended behind the Mig, quickly locked and shot a Python, getting his second kill.

The other two Migs had reversed, flying away from Wreckful's formation. In the span of 55 seconds, they'd downed three enemy aircraft and scared two others away.

Wreckful turned to follow the escaping Migs, when his number three crackled "bingo fuel" indicating his limit to return safely home. Wreckful slammed the throttle forward, as the Migs turned northwest. He locked a Sparrow on number one and pushed the button, only to watch the big aircraft roll and bank to the left, escaping the missile.

Wreckful stayed on the tail of number two of the Migs, which was now wiggling ahead, steeply descending to 5000 feet. Wreckful followed it, locked a Python on the hot tail, and seconds later watched as it exploded to a thousand pieces. He looked up and spotted the fifth Mig shining ahead. He pulled the stick up hard, and leveled behind the Mig when he reached its altitude. At this point the other pilots in his formation lost sight of Wreckful. When his radio crackled "where are you going?" he answered "heading 265," intentionally sending them off back to Israel, while he continued heading 340, on the last Mig's tail. He was too close to it for missiles, so he closed even more, his machine vibrating in the Mig's jet wash. He still managed to aim his sights on the target and release cannon fire. The rounds tore into the Mig, causing black chunks to break out into the wind. It turned upward, Wreckful in pursuit. It then leveled, flying more slowly due north, Wreckful following. After some time he advanced, positioned his plane closely parallel to the Migs left side and looked right to its cockpit. He then saw that the canopy was gone, and the pilot was nowhere around. He had chased an empty Mig for a considerable distance. *Wait till the guys hear this one!* He banked left heading 265, home. But when he checked the F-16s fuel gauge, he realized it couldn't make it.

8

Leora's heart palpitated with a pang at first sight of
two stern air force sergeants by her door next morning. She
uttered a short shriek, covering her face, as they quietly told
her, still grieving the loss of her first born son Guy 18 years
before, that her second son Avi was missing in action in
Iran. Atrocious images of Israeli captives tortured in Arab
prisons conjured in her mind, black horror awakening there
after few years of relative respite. She led the empathetic
sergeants out the door, closed it, walked slowly to her line
phone in the kitchen and called Michael Inbar, her ex-
husband. She heard him howling, his agony piercing her
ears. She dropped the phone and started sobbing savagely
and uncontrollably. Inbar called a high placed air force
intelligence officer that he flew with during his own combat
pilot service with the IAF. The man recounted Wreckful's
dogfights, informing that his last known coordinates were
latitude 51.7946°N, longitude 51.4741°E over Mamalu Bala,

high ground some 40 kilometers east of Tehran, concluding "Your son is an ace, Michael. Fireballs style of flying, but a bit of a rogue."

Leora had no notion how long she slumbered on the floor by the hanging phone when a soft knock awoke her. She stood up calmly, stepped to the door and opened it.

A young man about Avi's age stood there, smiling. He greeted her, "Good evening, Leora." She stood aside to let him in. He approached her from the porch, raised his right hand to touch her face and said "Know that your son Avi will be back with you, for Passover. Cleanse yourself and wait." She turned her head away, tears rushing in her eyes. When she turned back, he was gone. Who is this guy?

*

The rogue, object of his parents' great anxieties, was standing behind a pine tree about a 1600 kilometers away, holding his IAF issue revolver. Muffled voices of approaching men composited with the excited chirping of birds, and the rippling of water from a nearby stream. Some bird on the tree closest to Wreckful began singing three short low pitched notes bup, bup, bup, then louder ee-oh-lay, finally a rapid ventriloquial phrase. Then many birds joined in with their own repertoires.

Wreckful peeked around the tree, straight into the dark complexion of a man wearing a black leather jacket, cradling an automatic rifle, not two meters away. The man bounced sideways, swerving his weapon in Wreckful's direction, when the pilot's bullet hit his forehead.

Two other men standing apart in the open coniferous ground some 15 meters down from Wreckful's tree simultaneously fired at him. He leapt out, diving behind the fallen man's body, dropped his revolver, picked the man's rifle, shot one of the others down with a short burst, and submerged, two thumps muffled by the black jacket topping him following in split seconds' succession. He picked and placed the revolver in his flight jacket's left pocket, crawled back to the tree and stood up behind it, holding the rifle. He glimpsed around the tree and saw the man crouched in the open. The man fired a shot that whizzed by Wreckful's ear, then ducked to the ground, the pilot's salvo tearing into his right shoulder. Wreckful aimed for another shot at him, but refrained from shooting as the man's face dropped to the ground. He'd visibly lost consciousness, at least for a while.

9

"We reckon you've converged your airborne attack on three locations," the US Secretary of Defense said to his Israeli counterpart. "Do you plan to attack any other sites?"

"We've centered on Isfahan, where the Iranians produce uranium hexafluoride gas; Natanz, where they enrich that gas with thousands of centrifuges; and Arak, where they produce weapons grade plutonium with their heavy water research reactor. We may next attack their Qom site, located inside that mountain."

"Anything else?"

"If targeting data becomes available, other centrifuge fabrication sites. Such attacks would further stretch our already thinly strung capabilities, though. Maybe we'd decide not to expand the operations at this time."

They were conversing eye to eye in the office of the Israeli Minister of Defense in the ministry's building at the Kirya, located in central Tel Aviv. The American knew that Israel's F-15s and F-16s equipped with additional fuel tanks and refueled with KC-130 and 707 tankers in the beginning and the end of the planes' flights had reached their set targets, bombed them and returned to their bases. He also knew that a Boeing 777 sized remotely controlled unmanned aerial vehicle (UAV) bolstered the attack. "Did you use the GPS or laser versions for guiding those BLUs?" He was referring to the guidance systems of high energy bombs. The laser variant was more accurate, but required the placement of a special laser identification unit to spotlight target points.

"Natanz required the most accurate hits," The Israeli minister said, skipping the question. "The guidance system was good to allow our aircraft to propel their BLUs 15 kilometers from it, avoiding flights through the heavy Iranian air defenses. That target was largely under 23 meters of soil and concrete."

"Our intelligence is that you've damaged the targets severely," the American informed.

"The surface facility at Isfahan and reactor at Arak were completely destroyed. We know that the bombs burrowed on target at Natanz, and that the second and third bombs were accurately dropped into the cavities created by the first. We don't know yet whether the explosives had killed the centrifuges, or how many." Burrowing could penetrate the ceiling above the centrifuges, sometimes entirely collapse it.

"You stand about 70% chance of success, better of course if you've used the laser guided BLUs," the American paused in silence on that, to him a still obscure point, then asked "your casualties?"

"One F-15 shot down by air defense missiles at Arak, pilots instantly killed, and one F-16 lost out of fuel after a dogfight at Natanz."

"Yeah. I've heard the raves on that top gun. Great publicity for our combat aircraft. Any news about him?"

"Unheard from since he's parachuted east of Tehran."

"I'd have done everything to bring that one back. Come to think of it, if and when he does return, ask him to fly for us."

10

Wreckful ran from the scene of the gun battle, down a densely wooded area, stopping only when he reached a current of dark water flowing perpendicular to the hill. After a minute, he turned left and took off running down through vegetation along the water. He wasn't aware that some blood was dripping from his right ear, which had been buzzed by a bullet from the now unconscious man's gun.

Eighty five minutes later, Iranian army search teams reached that same man that Wreckful had left behind. A medic injected a greenish substance into his right arm from a large syringe. He opened his eyes. "Where did he go, " enquired the captain in charge, referring to the pilot whose parachute was earlier discovered a few kilometers farther up the mountainous area. "I was unconscious," the man muttered. "How long ago?" came the next question. "It was about fifteen thirty." The captain then ordered placement of check points in a 17 mile radius around the closest intersection down the main mountain road. He looked at his watch and said "about an hour and a half ago. Assuming he's advancing about five kilometers per hour, probably a young man at top physical form, he still couldn't be farther than 8 kilometers away." He yelled to his soldiers "Listen up. I want you to check every structure in a radius of seventeen kilometers from here. Look well also in open areas, and behind every tree. Keep in groups of five and be very alert as he's armed and lethal. Surround him when found and radio me. Look for a possible blood trail. Go go go."

Twenty five minutes later, Wreckful still running at the same athletic pace down the stream saw a small bridge over ahead. There was nobody around. He walked up the bank and over the bridge to the other side of the stream, turned left and resumed running down the right bank, stopping and slowing somewhat when he saw a small, shabby looking gas station through the brush.

At that time, a soldier radioed the Iranian captain, informing that his search dog has found a blood trail by the stream. "Go back, take three other soldiers with you, and get going following the dog on that," snapped the captain.

Lifting his head cautiously over the shrubs at the riverbank, Wreckful watched as a motorcyclist entered the gas station, drove to a pump closest, descended, leaned it on the tarmac and walked into the gas station. Wreckful laid the rifle down and walked casually to the station. The motorcyclist was still negotiating with the cashier there when the pilot entered the station area. Wreckful ran to the motorcycle, lifted it, kicked the starter and drove off onto the narrow mountain road, cranking it on his turn left almost as much as he did his aircraft, chasing that Mig some 35 hours before. He sped the bike on as fast as the snaking narrow road allowed. Eight minutes later he reached level ground and saw two trucks blocking the road, a score of soldiers standing around them. He swerved the bike right into a dirt road, hit a melon sized rock on it, and flew over the top into a field of two feet tall clumps of bulbous bluegrass.

By that time, the Iranian captain had gotten wind of the motorcycle hijacking, jumped onto a jeep, waited for two other soldiers to hop in, radioed for a helicopter to assist the chase and drove over to the gas station. Three minutes later he returned to the jeep with the soldiers and drove it left in the direction taken by the Israeli pilot, according to the station's cashier.

Wreckful stood up with some difficulty and examined the bike. It was a mess. He took off running down the field, the green sparklets scathing his legs. He stopped when he saw a barbed wired fence blocking the road ahead. He heard a screeching noise, pivoted around and saw an army jeep turning into the dirt road and stopping by the broken bike. An Iranian captain jumped out of it and called after Wreckful "you are surrounded. Put your hands up and walk slowly over here." Two other soldiers were running in his direction, guns aimed at him. Wreckful hesitated, only raising his hands when he saw the helicopter coming low overhead, a sniper seated at its widely open side door aiming his precision rifle straight at his face.

11

The two Iranian soldiers grabbed Wreckful under his armpits and pushed him toward their Captain waiting by the Jeep, framed by setting sun rays directly behind. Wreckful was blindfolded and pushed into the Jeep. The vehicle then started onto the road and took a left turn, to the South. Wreckful reckoned that it had traveled about 40 minutes Southbound when it stopped. He heard the Captain speaking to someone in Farsi, then the sound of a metal barrier opening up. The jeep moved forward in moderate speed, took a few turns left and right in sounds of military vehicles traffic and stopped again after about six minutes. One of the soldiers grabbed him again, and the other pushed him out of the Jeep. The Captain sputtered a command in Farsi. The two soldiers then grabbed Wreckful's arms and dragged him forward. Five seconds later he sensed he was inside a structure. He was spun to the right, led forward a few seconds more and made to stop. At the sound of a heavy metal door unlocking and opening, he was pushed forward. The eye cover was removed and the soldiers left, closed and locked the door behind him, leaving him blinking in a small, dark and shabby windowless cell. He sagged onto a naked stretcher by the dirty greyish scribbling spotted plaster wall and sank into a dreamless sleep.

*

Sixteen hundred kilometers to the west Inbar was
tailing his enigmatic young man in the suburb of East Talpiot,
Jerusalem. Inbar stood at street level by the corner of Olei
Hagardom and Avshalom Haviv streets, overlooking the subject
descending a flight of stairs to a concrete slab in the
courtyard of Dov Gruner street. The young man stood there a
few minutes, while Inbar was ruminating about his
investigation of the Jesus family tomb under that same
concrete slab, eighteen years back in time. The young man
then returned up the stairs, walked over to Inbar smiling as
always and proclaimed "at 9 PM tonight the power grid
would be suppressed at the military base of Parchin, where
your son Avi is held prisoner, and he will escape." Inbar
checked his Breitling, the time was 6:14 PM. When he
looked up again, the man was walking north toward the
Armon Hanatziv Promenade. Inbar hurried to follow him,
blurting "what did you say?" when he reached his side. But
the man continued roughly two hundred meters, to the edge

of the promenade, where they stood in silence side by side for several minutes. Inbar stared at the young man's profile, his subject viewing the Old City and Mount Zion straight ahead northward then slowly moving his regard slightly east to the Mount of Olives. "What's this place to you?" enquired Michael. "Google Talpiot bone box, preponderance of the evidence," he replied. He continued to gaze at the Holy City in silence until nightfall, then said "Farewell, Michael," and walked away. Inbar walked several hundred meters to the end of the promenade, turned into Naomi street and stopped by the door of a little restaurant, under a sign reading The Taverna. He used his cellphone to call Leora, then entered the place.

*

"Michael, who is that man?" Leora asked across a table under wooden beams inside the restaurant.

"I wish I knew," he said, forking a piece of kosher fish. "Certainly not a regular guy." Took him about 30 minutes to apprise her all his comings and goings around the fellow. It took her another 10 minutes to reveal her own physical encounter of the bewildering kind with the same person to Michael.

"Amazing, by what you've told me. How does he know where Avi is at this time?"

"He couldn't and doesn't. Probably one of these Kabbalah freaks that you waste too much time and money on."

"Do me a favor and check this out. God sometimes has mysterious ways."

Michael put his fork down, stood up grudgingly and walked out to the terrace of the restaurant. At that time of late evening there were no diners sitting there to view the spectacular panorama of the Jerusalem landscape and the Dead Sea. Michael called his IAF intelligence buddy.

"Do you know anything about downed electricity in Iran?"

"Can't talk about military operations over the cellphone," the man said.

"I'm not talking about the air attack two days ago, but about something to happen at 9 PM tonight."

"Nothing that I know of. Where?"

"Some place called Parchin. Supposedly a military base."

"You joking me. Michael? "

"Could you check that? My ex-wife is driving me nuts over this. Supposedly our son Avi is held prisoner there."

"This is bullshit, Michael. We have no intelligence where Wreckful is at this time."

"Check it out please buddy so I can enjoy the rest of my dinner," muttered Michael, "it isn't cheap." He replaced the cellphone into his pocket and returned to the table just when a waiter was lighting a fireplace next to it. "Done," he informed Leora. "Now eat that cold kosher fish staring at you. I wonder if it still remembers the sea it came from." She didn't laugh.

Five hours later at his Yemin Moshe apartment the line phone rang, "how the heck Michael did you know that?" the IAF man rustled via some static into Michael's ear.

"That, what?"

"That Parchin went completely dark at precisely twenty one hundred tonight. Still is."

"What was that about?" Rona asked when Michael replaced the phone in its cradle by their bed.

" An air force buddy told me about a total power failure at some military base in Iran."

"At this time of the night?" she examined his face. "What makes you so excited?"

"That young guy I'm shadowing told me about this earlier this evening, at six fourteen. He said this was going to happen at nine sharp, and so it did."

"This outreaches logic in every way."

"Wait till you hear this. That guy also said Avi is held prisoner in that same military base. And Leora says he's told her sometime ago that Avi would be back for Passover."

"Where did she tell you that, during the paranormal session at the Kabbalah institute?"

"Cut it out Rona, I'm as down to earth as you. The guy is better informed than I ever was. The air force could have used drones to disable the power grid over there."

"I've read we can do that. Probably did to facilitate the air attack that Avi participated in. But why would they do it tonight, two days later?"

"Hopefully to assist a commando operation to rescue Avi. Wow, that guy must have ears by the mouth of the IAF chief operations officer."

"My hunch Michael is that he gets his information from a higher authority. What was he doing at Talpiot?"

"Beats me. He said to Google 'Talpiot bone box preponderance of the evidence' when I asked him what the place was to him."

Rona stood up quietly after Michael fell asleep. She went to the open computer in the living room, googled the keywords and read a blog that discussed the magnitude of the find of what many consider had been Jesus' family tomb in Talpiot. The author substantiated a conclusion, as follows:

>"*Ask yourself a hypothetical question. If Talpiot tomb hadn't yet been found, how would Jesus' family tomb have looked, which ossuaries would it have contained, to when would it have been dated and where would it have been located? Even if, like me, you're not formally educated specifically in any field directly related to this subject, anyone with general education and common sense who's curious enough could educate himself to form a perfectly valid opinion. The critics of this find are also less than perfectly qualified for the task - they are either Israeli archeologists with no real knowledge of the New Testament and other Christian sources, or Christian scholars with no thorough knowledge of Hebrew, Judaism and Jewish Law. And none of them apparently has expertise in statistics, or they wouldn't advance the shallow argument that 'the names were common.' It's the cluster of names that's uncommon.*

I would have thought of a tomb just like the tomb we're discussing. It fits perfectly with what I'd have expected Jesus' family tomb to be. Right place, right period, right names. In addition, there is substantial evidence for this conclusion - having to do with symbology - that I expanded upon in 'The Bone Box.'

The foregoing doesn't mean that the Talpiot tomb is the real thing beyond reasonable doubt, only that if an unbiased jury were presented with all the evidence, pro and con, it could quite logically have concluded that it is indeed the last tomb of Jesus, by preponderance of the evidence."

Who is this guy?

12

Jangle stirred Wreckful. He opened his eyes to damp darkness. The commotion was coming from outside his cell. An unlocking sound came from the door. He tensed in the stretcher, fearful that he would be dragged for interrogation. Something rustled on the door, but it remained closed. The bustle subsided to further bedlam, punctured by occasional distant shouts. Then the door crinkled.

Wreckful got out of the stretcher and tip toed barefoot to the door. He could hear nothing outside. He turned the knob on the door and pushed it slightly. It opened quietly without any resistance. Wreckful peeped out but couldn't see anything. He stepped into the total darkness, stretched his hand to feel the wall by the door, and touched a light switch. He flicked it up. A single bulb lighted dimly above his head.

Wreckful was standing in the middle of a fairly long corridor. He was alone, as far as he could see in both directions by the murky, yellowish light. After a few seconds, he turned and carefully walked the corridor to the right. He moved stealthily along a succession of closed cell doors, reached a T shaped end and surveyed both directions of the corridor running perpendicular from there. He couldn't see the full length of corridor going to the right. He found a light switch and turned it up, but the light didn't come. He turned and walked to the left corridor, which was visible. But several doors on the corridor were blocked by a metal sliding fence. Wreckful could see an exit behind it, by the soft silvery light coming through. He started climbing to the top of the fence, looked around again, descended to the other side and walked through the exit, into a large square lit solely by the shining Snow Moon drifting silently in the cloudless sky. He heard voices of men approaching and stepped back into the building. The voices came nearer. He moved slowly to the first door to his right in the corridor, rotated the handle clockwise, pushed the door, snuck inside the room and closed the door again. The room was large, with a window opening to the square. Wreckful moved quickly to the wall on the right of the window, just as he heard the conversing men passing by. When their steps faded away, he turned around examining the room. It opened to a kitchenette with a humming refrigerator opposite the door and to a small bedroom facing the window. Nobody else was in the main room and the kitchenette. Wreckful tiptoed catlike by the moonlight coming through the window into the bedroom. Three double-decked cots stood there unoccupied at the three windowless walls. A flashlight on a nightstand by the bed closest to Wreckful reflected the faint moonlight. He walked over and picked it up, returning to the main room. He saw a closet on the wall beside the window, opened it, picked a pair of dark blue jeans, a plain black T shirt, and a grey leather jacket and changed to those from his IAF flight coveralls. He placed the flashlight in the jacket's pocket and chose a pair of black sneakers that seemed his size, which fit when he tried them on. He threw his coveralls into the dark back side of the closet, taking a brown plastic bag that was hanging there. He then shut the closet, walked over to the refrigerator, placed as much food as he could in the bag and exited the room back to the square.

13

Rona was perusing the second Ein Gedi Synagogue Aramaic inscription on her computer." *Check the names... let's see..Yose and Ezron and Hizziqiyu the sons of Halfi...Rabbi Yose the son of Halfi, Hiziqiyu the son of Halfi...*"she murmured to herself. A strange idea came to her. She brought up the blog about the Talpiot tomb she'd read the previous night, going over the ancient detailed names pertaining to the inscriptions on the bone boxes found there. "Here's another 'Yose', though that form for the name Yoseph is extremely unusual." She clicked back to the inscription then froze for a moment, and googled "Yose bar Halfi." On the first page that brought up links to the same inscription. She flipped through the Googled pages, then stopped with one of the partial hits, a translation into the Aramaic of the New Testament, named 'The Syriac New Testament." Rona went to her bookshelf. She picked out the New Testament, opened it at Acts 1:13 and read '...*Those present were Peter, John, James and*

Andrew; Philip and Thomas, Bartholomew and Matthew; James son of Alphaeus and Simon the Zealot, and Judas son of James." She examined the Aramaic text again. It referred to 'James son of Alphaeus' as 'Ya'acov bar Halfi.' Alphaeus was a transliteration into the Greek of the name Halfi. Her Aramaic was good enough to ponder that most probably came from the word for "sword." She remembered some studies she's read that connected several dots in two different Synoptic Gospels: a certain first century piece of papyrus, and a lost first century text quoted in a later text. The renowned scholars who authored these studies concluded that 'Alphaeus' was the same person as a 'Clophas' mentioned in other passages of the New Testament. And Clophas in turn was a brother of Jesus' legal father Joseph. Rona also knew that some Bible scholars suggest that 'James son of Alphaeus' was Jesus' oldest brother. Now she knew his real name was "Ya'acov bar Halfi.' Since 'Yose' was the precise nickname of Jesus' second brother according to one Gospel, then 'Yose bar Halfi' could have been his proper name. But Jesus and his brothers lived and died in the first century, and this 'Yose Bar Halfi' is mentioned very respectfully as an apparently generous donator for remodeling of the Ein Gedi Synagogue in the fourth century… She shut her computer down, contemplating what the connection could be.

Who is this guy?

14

Wreckful was walking around the large military base, by many different sorts of installations, structures, silos, bunkers, hangars, tunnels and what looked like entrances to underground structures. Everything was completely dark, except for soft whitish illumination from the heavens. With no light pollution, he easily identified the various constellations, the Milky Way and the North Star. He made mental note of the directions of each and every installation. Soldiers walked around, past and toward him several times, and military vehicles moved busily to and fro, but seemed to not particularly notice him. The electricity was obviously down in the entire base and they were working on that problem.

Walking past a group of large hangars, Wreckful noticed an airstrip stretching from some hundred meters straight ahead. A roadway on his right led into the cargo area and the general aviation apron site just behind it. He continued to walk casually forward about fifty meters when he reached a tie down general aviation apron lot. Two executive twin engine Learjets were parked there. He walked past that on an asphalt road next to a taxiway and reached a few small general aviation hangars. The door of one of the hangars was open wide. He approached the opening cautiously and stopped to listen. He heard nothing over the chirping of thousands of crickets all around him. He entered the hangar and lit his flashlight. There was a small office at the back of the structure. He walked over to it, saw it was empty, and pushed the door in. Hanging on a wall next to the door he saw a keychain with a small plastic key fob attached to the ring. It was marked by a plane's registration number. He took it into his pocket, and walked outside the hangar, to an old single engine Cessna 172 he saw tied there. The Cessna bore the registration number featured on the key fob. He untied the plane, walked over to the left door, opened it furtively, climbed to the left seat and started the engine, taxied the plane to the runway, stopped short of it, and revved the engine to check the gauges. Everything fine, fuel tank half full. He proceeded to the runway and pushed the throttle all the way in. The engine responded and the plane accelerated on the tarmac. At 70 mph airspeed Wreckful pulled the stick up, held the left rudder in just a tad with his foot, and went into the cloudless night sky. He turned the stick to the right while climbing, and passed over a small town that seemed normally lit. The lights of Tehran rolled out to his left as he was climbing. When the Cessna reached 6000 feet he reduced rpm to 75% of power and lowered the stick a bit to level the plane, steadied speed at 110 knots and took a north westerly direction, heading 340.

Wreckful was flying somewhat low relative to the terrain, wary of enemy fighters that might appear any moment to shoot him down. He reckoned that the Parchin radar would be dead out of electricity. He was unaware that in fact all over central and northwestern Iran military radar technicians were baffled by their screens, which were showing no planes at all, then flickering to blip hundreds of planes. Someone or something has bluffed the country's air defense radars, facilitating Wreckful's run.

Thirty minutes later Wreckful turned the Cessna left, to fly due West. With the plane banking gently he took in a wide view of a sea of lights blazing at him from Tehran a few kilometers to the South, the full moon some 30 degrees above on the right framing the scene. He leveled the wings when the direction gauge came to heading 270. With the wing fuel tanks half full, the Cessna's range would be around 250 nautical miles. Always upbeat, Wreckful expected to make it.

15

At the Oasis of Al Ahsa, Saudi Arabia, about sixty kilometers inland from the Persian Gulf, diners in the patio of a posh restaurant at the InterContinental were enjoying the beauty of the Snow Moon, looming to their west. Suddenly they saw a huge explosion about 100 feet above the horizon, then two more. Bits of glowing metal fell to the ground, setting fire to installations at Ghawar, the largest oil field in the world. Many of the workers occupying barracks at the oil field were also eating dinner, relaxing and sleeping when the explosions occurred.

An ambulance driver who'd arrived there minutes later described the scene on Saudi state TV: "The barracks area looked like a battleground. About ten vehicles were blown apart in the parking lot. Fire Department trucks were blasting sirens. Police then came and started clearing unhurt workers from the area for fear of a second wave of explosions. I saw some mutilated bodies lying about the grounds. Then our paramedics picked three badly wounded men and we transported them to the nearest hospital. We heard the nurses there saying two other victims of the attack in very critical condition were also brought to that hospital and just died of their wounds. I've later heard from work friends that three victims were in emergency surgery. Five were in various intensive care." "Over 180 persons were treated in six different hospitals," the TV anchor reported gravely. "These attacks were carried out by Iranian Shihab missiles. Shihab and Scud attacks also occurred concurrently in Kuwait, Qatar, Bahrain, the United Arab Emirates and Oman."

Three hours later, special operations command at McDill Airfoce Base, Florida, received orders to prepare Delta attack Force for operations aiming to destroy Shihab and Scud missiles in Iran.

16

The sun rising behind was projecting the little plane's silhouette moving westward on the semi arid landscape below. Colors of the barren hills were rapidly turning rosier every minute.

Wreckful checked his fuel gauge and looked down his left window, searching a suitable place to land. A river was snaking there in a generally westerly direction, the brush around it waving away from the approaching plane. The terrain was ragged. Wreckful rolled the plane 35 degrees to the right, to examine the other side of the river. A medium width road was following it. He reduced power, lowered the nose and flew diagonally across the road. It was empty at this early morning time. He then pulled the throttle out to idle the engine and turned left diagonally to the road. Checking left and right he verified it was still clear, made another ninety degree left turn into the mild wind coming from the Caspian Sea, applied his flaps and landed on the road, using his brakes to slow the plane, then touching the right rudder pedal slightly to turn into a small branching dirt road, where he stopped, choked the engine out, exited the plane and stood there, the soft wind waving his golden curls and the glowing sunrays flushing his face. After several minutes, he retrieved the brown plastic bag from the plane and walked to the bank of the river. There he sat and ate from it, with good appetite.

From that point on proceeding west along the river became an unmatched test of endurance that many others less trained and fit than Wreckful would have renounced because of the insidious natural enemies present. He was walking along the northern bank, carrying his brown plastic bag, buzzed and bitten by thousands of pesky mosquitos. His eyes dazzled with the blinding bright light reflected from the river. The ground was muddy of recently melted snow. The rocks were slippery and became hot even through the wet soles of his sneakers, as he waded in the muck. Still he preferred the lower riverbank over the parallel road due to its much reduced visibility and the immediate availability of clear, fresh water. Then with the lengthening shadows came the sudden cold, turning his cloths into freezing wet blankets on his skin already tormented with the innumerable mosquito bites. He still continued to walk in the moonlight for several hours. Stopping by a naked tree, he lay down under it and fell soundly asleep.

*

Early the next morning a policeman riding a motorcycle eastbound near where Wreckful had landed saw the Cessna stationed on the dirt road. He veered right off the main road, dismounted by the little aircraft and radioed the unique alphanumeric string that identified it, as painted on the fuselage. The officer at the station taking the report instructed his secretary to begin a search for all details about the plane. She switched her computer to the Iranian Aircraft Registration Inquiry database, and started working through eight different queries, which provided information about current registered owners, documents filed, aircraft dealers, and more.

17

Wreckful woke up on the early morning of his fourth day by the river loathe to begin another march in the unwelcome company of thousands of blood-sucking flying pests, already buzzing in his ears. He pulled the brown plastic bag to him. It had one piece of stale bread. Munching on it, he walked over to the river, cupped ice cold water over his head, gulped another handful and set out west again. But on that day he got lucky. After he'd walked about two hours downriver he saw a row boat in the mud two hundred meters from him, and ran over to it, excited to find two oars and one fish bait under the deck head. He pushed the wooden boat to the water, jumped in and began rowing with a weak current, thankful to the mosquitoes that must have driven the owner away. The chilly rain drizzling over was creating a rainbow in the western sky ahead. The birds chirping and the sound of the river were truly tranquil around him.

Wreckful advanced that way with the river boarded by craggy cliffs for four days, eating the delicious fish he'd caught, sushi style, and stopping to sleep wherever he could secure the boat by either of the banks. On the fifth day of this easy floating, heavy rain came on the ragged hills, and a torrent of water flash flooded the river. By early evening the rush was pushing the little row boat faster than the pilot reckoned he could safely handle. He rowed across white wavelets toward the flat left bank. The little boat then hit a rock and the hull broke. Wreckful jumped into the cold water and managed to swim to safety by the wiry brush plants growing from the wet gravel there. He stood up and looked around him. He couldn't see across the gorges at right bank of the river. But when he scrutinized the unobstructed view to the left, he saw lights indicating a settlement. He started walking south toward the lights. After ten minutes he came to an asphalt road with a sign in Arabic and English scripts, the latter reading "*Miyaneh 7 km.* " He continued walking southbound, following the arrow on the sign.

*

Back in Parchin the erstwhile Iranian Captain who'd caught the Israeli pilot, sitting at his office desk, received a phone call informing him that the Cessna stolen from the base had been found. He walked to the large map hanging on his wall and examined the given location, stood thinking in silence for two minutes and then muttered "Qezel Owzan." The name of the river. He called two of his lieutenants to his office, shut the door and instructed them to monitor all police reports for unusual incidents in places along the river, west of the location where the plane was found.

18

Around midnight two US Army Blackhawk
helicopters of the 160th Special Operations Aviation Regiment
carrying eight Delta Force commandos ascended from the
USS Bataan in the Persian Gulf off the coast of the United Arab
Emirates. They flew low over the sea and then continued at
high speed and low attitude toward the hiding place of
Iranian Scud launchers located minutes earlier by a Special
Air Forces hunter team somewhere in Southern Iran. Two
hours later they landed in the dark, discharging the
commandos in two Fast Attack Vehicles (FAV). The vehicles
carried food, water, ammunition, extra fuel, anti tank
missiles and mounts for grenade launchers. One of the
vehicles carried a 30mm cannon, the other carried a heavy
machine gun. The vehicles then started moving northbound
on the harsh terrain. After they've covered 47 miles, the
driver of the lead vehicle saw several sets of headlights
moving perpendicularly to him about a mile ahead. He
turned the FAV to a cluster of tall bushes on his right side
and stopped it there. The second FAV followed.

The commando leader observed the headlights with night vision binoculars, and saw Iranian Army trucks crossing a small metal bridge over a dry wadi. "Sentries," he muttered, looking to the right of the bridge. There were several trucks and army tents yards beyond that. "Machine guns... troops... military vehicles. Follow me." He crouched and ran down the wadi on his right, then proceeded silently toward the bridge, followed closely by the other commandos. When they reached shouting distance from the sentries they stopped and moved stealthily behind a large boulder by some lowly trees. One of the Iranian sentries heard leaves crackling, gazed to the boulder's direction through his night vision device, and spotted the binoculars of the leader, who at this time was whispering "the Scuds mounted on their TELs are camouflaged to the right of the tents." The sentry directed a searchlight on the boulder just as two of the special forces fired anti tank missiles at the Transport Erector Launches of the Scuds. Seconds later, a heavy gunfire erupted between the Iranians and the Delta Force company, just when the Scuds exploded, the ensuing fire lighting the battle scene.

Having killed many of the enemy, the commandos ran back in the wadi to their FAVs and started driving them back as fast as they could. Minutes later they saw a road sign in Farsi. The leader instructed his driver to take the direction per the arrow. Twenty seconds later they were driving southbound on a two lane asphalt road. But 18 miles down they saw an Iranian tank blocking that road, two other tanks flanking its sides turning their cannon turrets toward them. "Jump," the leader yelled as he leapt out of his FAV. The other commandos followed. They were all running off the right lane toward a crag as the FAVs exploded in quick succession behind them.

19

Wreckful reached the outskirts of Miyaneh before dawn, having passed through the destroyed middle of an ancient arched stone bridge a minute earlier. He was still soaking wet, though the rain now subsided to a drizzle. He reached a street branching into the town on his left and walked along it until he came to a wet unpaved square surrounded by two and three level red brick buildings. Most of them had little open fruit shops at ground level. Some carts standing around also carried fruit.

Wreckful walked over to a shop that looked busier than others, took an orange into his leather jacket pocket and walked away. But the vendor caught that, brandishing a wad of cash and calling after him in a language that sounded like Turkish to him. He walked back to the shop, extended his right arm over the fruit stall to the vendor, nabbed the cash he was holding and put it in his jacket's pocket. Wreckful then turned and walked away from the dumbfound vendor toward a narrow street on the right side of the fruit bazaar. He then perceived a policeman coming after him. He turned left into an alley and ran straight forward on puddled ground. Reaching a main street, he soon came to a small bus terminal. He would have entered it to take a bus, but the policeman was still chasing. Wreckful continued running forward. A minute later he reached the highway and turned left on it. Glancing back he saw the panting policeman stopping behind him, barking into his walky-talky. He ran about three minutes more when he reached a train station. Looking back now he saw two policemen on bicycles following him less than a hundred meters back. He sprinted to a modern style bridge over the railway, where a long freight train was proceeding northbound, reached it 29 seconds later, mad jumped over the low metal fence onto the roof of a boxcar. He then rolled on his back and waived to the policemen gunning at him from the quickly distancing bridge.

20

A white sheep was grazing the dry brush next to a ditch in southern Iran; its little shepherd came to pick it up. He then saw a black net strung over the ditch and stepped cautiously forward to examine the strange thing. He turned and ran back in panic when he saw a pair of eyes staring back at him from a dirt smeared face.

The Delta Force man moved the net, stood and aimed his rifle at the boy's back. But he didn't shoot. "What was that?" another soldier asked from the spider hole. "Little boy, like ten years old. Probably thinks he saw a Jinni." The other soldier grunted, "I thought we were well hidden here."

They'd reached the farmland area three hours earlier, before sunrise, alternately running and walking close to four hours in the night. They dug the spider hole to hide out during the day in wait for the helicopters that would come to take them back to base at night. Their hideout now accidentally discovered by the kid, they moved to a long irrigation ditch several hundred yards away, set a parameter there, and held watchfully. Hours passed in tense silence, but nothing happened. They thought they were safe, sat down and ate from their provisions. But they soon noticed armed Iranian militias approaching their position. The company commander radioed his base for close air support and emergency evacuation. Minutes later three Predator drones took off back in the United Arab Emirates and flew out to rescue the Delta Force team. At that time the commandos were pointing their weapons at the militias, trying to no avail to scare them away. The Iranians instead moved closer around the ditch. Several trucks stopped nearby discharging scores of soldiers. The commandos realized they were in real trouble. They ran down the ditch in the opposite direction of the trucks but reached a dead end 300 yards away. There being nowhere else to go, they moved to fighting positions in the four foot deep round ditch, prepared to counter an assault. Several additional Iranian army trucks stopped by the first trucks and another infantry platoon came out. Then started shooting at the Americans, who shot back.

At that point one of the three pilots of the approaching drones radioed the commandos saying he can't see them. "Can you see the trucks, we're in a ditch about 500 yards east of them," the commander said. The Iranian soldiers were closing in. The radio cackled "can't position you yet." The commander said "I'll take the risk, shoot at the soldiers now." Two missiles carrying cluster bomblets came from the first drone, hitting the Iranians not 200 yards from the ditch. Many fell, but most of the platoon lay on the ground shooting at the commandos. The latter tried to hold the platoon off, fiercely shooting back. Most of the Iranian soldiers resumed their advance. At that point from the flashes the Air Force analyst in Indiana figured out the direction the Iranians were firing, and found the ditch, where he observed the flashes coming from the Americans' guns. He notified the drone pilots. When the Iranian soldiers were just about 40 yards away from the commandos the lead drone pilot said "I have it, I can see your ditch now," the other two drones then fired four missiles that discharged their lethal bomblets a few yards above the Iranians, The Americans ducking for dear life in the ditch. Ten seconds later, when the commander peeped out, all the enemy he saw were lying dead in the field. At nightfall two Blackhawks landed next to the dead and whisked the Delta Force team across the Persian Gulf back to base.

21

Wreckful was munching on his stolen orange, enjoying the view around him. The train was moving westbound on a long bridge, crossing a large lake divided into north and south parts by a causeway that the train had just traveled. The lake extended in both directions as far as he could see. He watched a flamingo that took off from a small rocky island flying low over the deep blue water toward a large residential island at the eastern part of the lake. A smell of sulfur, like rotten eggs, tanging the air reminded Wreckful of the Dead Sea. He threw the orange peels to the morning haze and watched them fall, barely budging the heavy water.

*

Back in Parchin the Iranian Captain was perusing the reports of incidents along the Qezel Owzal river his lieutenants had collected, when a particular report about a transient jumping on a train from a bridge at Miyaneh caught his attention. Why the hell would anyone risk his life over an orange? He instructed his secretary to email the police station in that town a video clip taken by the security cameras in the base. "Tell them to find out if that was the same man. Also email the pilot's photo to police, Basji and MOIS in all railway stations and towns along the westbound routes from Miyaneh," he added to the intercom and reclined back in his leather armchair.

22

The Eged bus from Tel Aviv to *Metula*, the
northernmost town in Israel, was travelling at the foot of
the hills just north of the ancient site of Migdal. Daniela
Inbar sitting by a left side window watched the high cliffs of
Mount Arbel. The bus driver started negotiating the narrow
turns uphill, midday sunlight reflecting from the waters of
the Sea of Galilee back to his right. Several minutes later the
bus stopped at Capernaum. The young man who'd boarded
that morning after her at the central station of Tel Aviv
enunciated "come with me Daniela,'" and descended. She
stood up and followed in his steps.

He walked down the road leading to the site. He
came first to a Greek Orthodox church with white domes
and waited there for her. Then they entered the church. He
walked around it, gazing at the various paintings on the
wall. After half an hour he led Daniela out and to the right.
They walked about 50 meters and came to the ruins of an
ancient synagogue. "I haven't seen this before," he
muttered, inspecting the columns and reading some of the
ancient inscriptions. "There was an earlier synagogue
here," he motioned at the partially broken western wall. He

then turned around. Indicating a hexagonally shaped building resting on short pillars across the walkway to the south he said "Simon Peter's home was here, under this newly constructed Franciscan Church." He led her to the shore of the lake, lowest freshwater body on Earth. "Levi Matya the son of Halfi was sitting here, collecting customs and other taxes," he said. Then he turned left walking eastward along the shore with her, until they reached the entrance point of the river Jordan. Here he stopped and looked up the river to the north.

Daniela looked to the same direction, observing a beautiful eagle that rested on an extended tree branch that hung over the river. The eagle took off and flew in the Jordan's river path, coming down in a spectacular rush.

The young man took Daniela's hand and they walked together back to the bus station.

Who is this guy?

23

Thirty five minutes after crossing the bridge over
the lake, the freight train entered a station marked "Urmia."
Wreckful cautiously climbed down the boxcar's left side to
a concrete platform, and walked to the station's building. A
surveillance technician seated in the second floor of the
building identified him on his monitor. Wreckful observed
a door marked with the familiar men's public restroom
symbol and entered it. He washed his face and armpits,
accessed the toilet closest to the restroom's door, shut the
unlockable toilet's door and sat, responding to nature's call.
Soon he heard excited clamor of men entering the
restroom. He pulled his pants up zipping them and stood
on the toilet. A second later the toilet's door opened slowly
and a policeman cautiously peeped inside. Wreckful leaped
from the toilet, dropping the policeman to the floor,
instantly grabbed the gun he was holding and shot another
policeman standing next to the urinals two meters away.
Wreckful knocked the first policeman unconscious with a
deft elbow blow to the temple, sprang to the restroom's
door, slammed it out and sprinted to the building's main
entrance, gun in hand. Thousands of protesters were rallied
in the broad street to call on the Iranian government to save
the dying Urmia Lake, which the pilot had crossed less than
an hour earlier. He put the gun in his jacket's inside pocket

and ran into their midst. A few minutes later a violent clash began between rally participants and security forces. Police shot tear gas at the crowd. Wreckful stepped out of the multitude, turned into a side street opposite the railway building and walked quickly away from the scene.

*

Back in Parchin, the Captain was informed of the incident. Twenty minutes later he boarded a Learjet and flew to Urmia.

24

Wreckful reached a large bus terminal. He entered inside, walked over to a large board indicating departures from Urmia in Farsi and English and then strolled to the ticket window. "One way to Van," he pronounced in English. The ticket agent asked something in a foreign language that again sounded Turkish to him. "Tourist," responded Wreckful, handing over cash. He took the ticket, bought sandwiches and soda cans at a shop and walked over to the platform indicated on the departure information board. He stood under a sign in Farsi, munching a sandwich and glancing around for any suspicious movement. But nothing unusual happened. Twenty minutes later a bus moved into the slot and he boarded it without incident. After seven minutes the driver started the engine and drove the bus out to a busy street.

*

Forty minutes later the Captain deplaned from the Learjet at Urmia Airport with his two lieutenants. They hopped on an army Jeep that drove them to the train station. Having inspected the video clip of the pilot sprinting out, he snapped to his lieutenants, "Check all security videos taken in land transport stations located inside a radius of four kilometers around here. Go go go."

25

The bus traveled northbound on a highway that turned westbound after about a hundred fifty kilometers, heading toward a barren ridge that bisected the highway from northwest to southeast. When they reached a few kilometers from the foot of the mountains the bus slowed, then stopped with the traffic. Wreckful saw a checkpoint ahead. A soldier was proceeding in their direction, stopping to inspect every vehicle. In fifteen minutes he reached the bus, stepped onto it, said a few words to the driver, looked back at the passengers, descended and waived the driver forward. The bus moved after the other cleared vehicles, the barrier ahead lifted and the bus accelerated westbound again. Five minutes later it was crawling up a craggy ridge, reaching the top in ten minutes, descending faster several hundred meters to the foot of a parallel ridge in the desolate landscape, up and down again and again. This nauseating wavelike voyage continued for several hours, until the bus stopped once more in view of a checkpoint flying an Iranian flag on top of another peak. Two militia men advanced directly to the bus flashing their guns and shouting at the driver. The door then opened, they boarded the bus rapidly, immediately swerved toward the passengers and pointed their automatic rifles at Wreckful's face. He ducked behind the passenger before him and drew the gun from his jacket's inside pocket as a bullet whizzed past, hitting a woman in the rear of the bus. Wreckful then rolled into the floor of the aisle, raised his gun with both hands and shot the militia men dead before any of them could make another move. He stood up, ran to the open bus door, jumped out and sprinted down and off the road to his right, where he was invisible from the checkpoint. He heard excited shouts mingled with gunfire behind him and continued sprinting on the dry pathways until the rays of the setting sun began to blind him and nobody was pursuing him anymore. He slowed his running pace, reduced it to a walk and stopped after twenty some seconds. He sat on a boulder by the path, lifted his head and gazed at the first star that appeared in the sky dome above.

*

Thousands of miles away at the National Reconnaissance Office (NRO) in the United States a technician locked a spy satellite on Wreckful gazing at the sky. The technician has followed the pilot several hours back, after he'd noticed a solitary figure sprinting away from a group of Iranian soldiers and Basji militia then running for hours on ragged terrain of the mountain chain of Zargos, at the Iran-Turkey border. He zoomed on Wreckful's face and took several pictures of it, activating an identification query. Seconds later a positive match was found with a picture taken of the Israeli top gun from when he'd trained in a US air force base on the most advanced long range version of F-16 fighter jets.

26

"Nothing dystopian in the Middle East yet," declared the US Director of National Intelligence in an office overlooking lower high-rise buildings at Manhattan. His Israeli counterpart nodded, "certainly not spiraling out of control. The region hasn't transformed to anything new yet."

"But our efforts to destabilize the government may succeed, General."

"Not game-changing yet, I'm afraid. Many of the high officials still alive in Iran are hiding; thousands of Iranians are protesting in Tehran. But we estimate the theocracy will nevertheless hold. They still have a majority support base in the rural towns and villages."

"We're not halfway done."

"I hope no more missiles destabilize the Arab free riders along the Gulf."

"You certainly should, seeing that the Saudis have turned a blind eye to your attack jets overflying their territory on their way to those nuclear facilities."

"Your special operations against Shihab and Scud launch facilities are apparently very successful, "the Israeli said, skipping the overfly remark.

"Indeed they were, though we had a really hard time rescuing one Special Forces unit."

"Yeah, I know about that."

"Well, seems like you know more about our soldiers than yours, General." The American took a photograph out of his drawer and put it on the desk. "Here's a little parting present. This pilot should run the Marathon in the next Olympics."

"Where was that taken?" The Israeli Major General exclaimed, staring at Wreckful's upturned face in the picture. *Inbar's middle son*, he thought. *Thank you God for not turning my old buddy into another Job. He's suffered enough with his first son's death.*

"Somewhere in the mountains on the border between Iran and Turkey. We'll give you the exact coordinates."

"Well, look at the bright side. We must have given him a good briefing of the escape routes from Iran."

"Not to mention survival training. We would have done anything to get this one back and flying."

"He soon will."

27

Daniela and the young man were dining at a restaurant in Jerusalem on a rooftop of Yemin Moshe. "You never told me your name," she said.

He took in the panoramic view of Sultan's Pool. Looking beyond the pool at Mount Zion and the Benedictine contours of the Dormition Abbey, built on the site where Mary is said to have drifted off to eternal sleep, and at the Cenacle, considered traditionally the very room of the Last Supper, located beyond the Dormition Abbey above David's Tomb,."Call me Josiah," he announced. "Josiah ben David."

"Tell me more about yourself."

"There's nothing much to tell, Daniela."

"Computers is my life. What's driving you?"

He gestured solemnly around, and pronounced "by the hand of His Messiah God may glorify Himself in front of His enemies. He will overthrow Belial's Legions, the Seven nations of Vanity, and by the hand of the Poor Ones of His Redemption, with the fullness of His Wondrous Power, He has opened a Gate of Hope to the cowering heart. He will kindle the Downcast in Spirit who shall be as a flaming torch in the chaff to ceaselessly consume Evil until Wickedness is destroyed."

Later that night in her apartment Daniela googled "Josiah ben David." That didn't bring up any contemporary person. She switched to the Interior Ministry's database of the Israel Population Registry, entering the same search. The monitor didn't return any information. Instead it now flickered, "Please enter your password." She started her cracking system, involving sending a key logger to a computer at the local Interior Ministry branch. The following morning an official was checking his records on that computer. Daniela looked through her key logs, knowing that if someone had accessed it she would find the password. Thousands of code numbers were now running down the screen. She sifted through, looking for something resembling a password and found some letter-number combinations that had been entered on the computer. Trying one of the combinations the computer returned "Incorrect password. For security reasons, your account will be locked after two more incorrect attempts." She tried the next one. The computer blinked "highly confidential." She stood up, gazing at the computer. The file there contained a single brief entry "born April 7, 1983." She proceeded in the same way to break into the databases of many government offices that would have information about any resident in Israel, alive or dead. The Ministry of Transportation for driver's license; the Ministry of Health for live birth and hospitalization records; the Ministry of Justice for court reports; the Ministry of Culture for pupil names. She continued with private institutions' databases: colleges, universities, hospitals. Everything she could think of and manage to break into. There was no information. Nothing at all.

At noon Daniela picked up her cellphone and called her father.

Who is this guy?

28

A helicopter whirring low woke Wreckful. He turned to the direction the noise was coming from and blinked at the daylight. As his sight focused the sound subsided. A minute later it was dead calm again all around the cave he'd slept in. He sat up, ate and drank from the provisions he'd taken at the bus station in Urmia, then stood up and walked toward the source of the light at the opening of the cave. Coming out he cupped his hand on his forehead and examined the sky, then resumed marching westward on the hard soil in complete solitude.

Two hours later, when he was advancing along a wadi, a rumble came from behind the bleached cliff to his left. He dropped to the ground just as an Iranian army helicopter appeared and hovered directly above. A familiar voice then called through a loudspeaker, "Impressive, Colonel, that you've made it to here. You must surrender now." Wreckful rolled over on his back and stared up at the barrels of two sniper rifles and the smiling face of that Iranian Captain, just when the helicopter exploded, its burning pieces falling all around him.

Wreckful marched for four more hours, when he saw a horse rider approaching from the west. *Another one to drop*, he thought. *This is becoming ridiculously violent.* He drew out the gun from his breast pocket and blustered at the horseman, "now where the hell do you come from?"

"Turkey," the man answered, pointing his index back at a border pole, not 200 meters away.

*

Three days later back in Jerusalem Leora picked up the ringing phone. "Hi Mom," her son's voice came. "What's up?"

"Avi!" she exclaimed. "Where are you?"

"At our Embassy in Ankara. Brand new. Remodeled when the Ambassador returned, courtesy of the new Turkish government."

"Say again, darling. Are you in Turkey?"

"Of course. I'm going to sleep now. Need some rest. I'll be with you for the Seder."

Before Passover. Just as that young man foretold, she raved.

29

Four days later the Director of National Intelligence received a phone call from Israel on his scrambled line, "You calling to thank me for that photo, General?" he said.

"Exactly. I'm flying to New York tonight. How's your schedule for tomorrow?"

"Come at noon, we'll go to lunch."

As it happened they had their lunch in the Director's high-rise office on the next day. The purpose of the meeting was discussion of information elicited from Wreckful's observations at Parchin. Over a year earlier, The International Atomic Energy Agency (IAEA) had identified a large steel container structure there. They concluded Iran had used it for conducting experiments for an implosion device. To "*create a blast wave that compresses a central ball of nuclear fuel into an incredibly dense mass, so that a chain reaction can be started, ending in a nuclear explosion.*" That would be used to reduce the size of an atomic bomb so it could fit as warhead on a Shihab-3 missile. The Israeli analysts who've examined the information concluded that the Iranians now had one or more such central balls ready. That would give them the ability to fire ballistic missiles at Israel and Europe. The United States could be next.

"Thanks General. I'll pass the raw details for analysis here," the Director said. "Do your experts believe the devices are still in Parchin?"

"Affirmative, though they may have already transferred one or two to other hiding places."

"We'll double check that, General."

"Of course."

"It's really a good thing we helped you locate that pilot with that photo."

"Thanks also for exploding that Iranian helicopter. That got him out of a very tight spot."

"Come on, you don't need to thank us for your own show, General."

"Trying to puzzle me? If Israel had anything to do with that timely explosion, nobody has bothered to get me into the picture."

The Director chuckled, "Act of God, then?"

30

On the next Monday, Leora hosted the Seder, a ritual feast that marks the beginning of Passover, which has been performed by Jews for about three millennia. Michael Inbar was sitting at the head of the stylized dinner table set for the Seder, flanked by Leora, Avi and Daniela on his left, Rona and their son Jonathan on his right.

Michael started reading aloud the Haggada, the ancient text that retells the story of the Exodus from Egypt, following the Biblical command: "You shall tell your child on that day, saying, 'It is because of what the LORD did for me when I came out of Egypt.' " Each member of Michael's family around the table participated alternatively reciting parts of the text in Hebrew and Aramaic.

Toward the end of the ceremony, after a third cup of wine was poured, Daniela walked to the front door, opened it as part of the tradition for the Prophet Elijah and gasped at the face of the young man, joyfully smiling to her from the porch. Then she took him by the hand back to the table, and said "this is my friend Josiah ben David." As he sat down at her right next to the wine cup reserved for Elijah,

Rona said. "I believe we've all met him, but now we get his name. Most gloriously royal, the tragically heroic king of Judah."

Here she goes again, Michael reflected. *To me the better analogy is Elijah. Almost as elusive.* But after the ceremony ended Rona acted again on her insatiable curiosity, addressing Daniela's apparently close friend. "I've read that blog essay about the Talpiot Tomb. What's your take on the adjacent tomb?"

"It's the tomb of Nakdimon ben Gorion's family."

"You mean the same person whose name is transliterated in the New Testament into Greek as Nicodemus?"

"I don't know about that. He was fabulously rich."

"True, the Talmud is full with anecdotes about this fact."

"I don't know that, either."

Rona left the table, stepped over to a bookshelf on the wall behind the young man, took a heavy volume of the Babylonian Talmud, sat by his side and opened it. She leafed for a minute, then indicated, "Here's one of the anecdotes. Ketubot 66a-b." He leaned over that while she read aloud:

> *"The daughter of Nakdimon ben Gorion*
> *was once allotted by the sages four*
> *hundred gold coins daily for her perfume*

basket she told them give such judgment
to your daughters they said Amen."

He laughed, "Deference wasn't exactly Miriam's best trait. It didn't happen exactly like this says but she was indeed allotted what everyone else considered very much money after her divorce."

"There are several other similar stories about Nakdimon's great wealth in the Talmud and other ancient sources. Come to think of it, makes much sense for him to occupy the closest tomb to Jesus' family. He probably believed that would best assure he'd be among the first to rise from the dead. Do you concur, Josiah?"

He didn't respond to that. Who is this guy?

31

Inbar woke up late on the next morning. He called his secretary, already in the office at the district police headquarters on the Russian compound in Jerusalem, and asked her to arrange a meeting with Zalman Ganot of the Israel Antiquities Authority. A few minutes later she called back, "Ganot asks what for, Michael." "Close encounters of the paranormal kind," he grunted. A minute later the secretary set an appointment around noon at the Eretz Israel museum in Ramat Aviv, a suburb of Tel Aviv.

Traffic was light that holiday morning on the main highway to the city that never stops, sixty kilometers down by the Mediterranean Sea. Inbar got there ahead of time. He entered the main building of the historical and archaeological museum, asked for Ganot and was directed to proceed on a westbound path outside that building. Two minutes later he spotted the IAA man standing in the open surrounded by ancient sundials. "Long time no see, " the latter said, extending his hand. "What query brings you to me, something relating to the Haggadah? I'm afraid I don't know the location of Moses' tomb."

"Cut the chit-chat, Zalman. I want to know what happened to the bones in the Talpiot boxes, back around this same holiday in 1980."

"Why suddenly now?"

"There's this strange ET figure dating my daughter… he takes unordinary interest and knows amazingly much about that Tomb. I need to dig into what happened." He went on to tell Ganot the facts substantiating his request. The archaeologist then began a bizarre account. They were both unaware of the middle-aged woman who was recording their conversation from behind an Iron Age large round millstone about forty meters south of them.

An hour later in Langley, Virginia a CIA analyst pressed the play button on his computer, listening to the recording. It all came out nice and clear.

Ganot: "You probably know by now that in deference to religious precepts, human remains found in ossuaries are usually given Jewish burial as soon as possible."

Inbar: "Yeah, you'd told me that back in 1995."

Ganot: "The law prescribes that skeletal remains found in ossuaries be reburied."

Inbar: "That too. But you added then that 'Sometimes, in special findings, they're not.'"

Ganot: "Perfect memory. That's basically what happened with the subject bones."

Inbar: "Now we're talking. Spill the beans on that."

Ganot: "After the bone boxes were transferred to our storage facility we started cleaning them. The lead archeologist became excited and worried that he'd found the real thing."

Inbar: "I know all about that. I've heard his wife's later account during that special conference at Jerusalem in 2007."

Ganot: "Anyway, on the next day the Hevra Kadisha came and cleaned out the remains."

Inbar: "Obviously. Is that all?"'

Ganot: "Except for one detail. Before the remains from one particular burial box were touched, some other men came to the place to take them. The orthodox Hevra Kadisha protested. But then the leader of the new guys produced an order from the highest authority, so we let them proceed. They carefully collected the bones from the ossuary into a plastic container and drove away with it."

Inbar: "And which particular bone box was that?"

Ganot: "The one inscribed 'Yeshua bar Yehosef'."

Jesus son of Joseph.

32

Inbar and Ganot were having lunch at one of several fish restaurants lining the promenade at Tel Aviv's harbor area when a whoosh sound followed by a loud explosion stirred them.

"What the hell was that?"

Inbar pointed his index at a small general aviation airport to the north. "Eat your fish, Zalman," he growled. "Don't worry about these sundials. The smoke is coming from Sde Dov."

"Breaking news" then appeared on the bottom of a television screen fixed to the restaurant wall opposite their table. An anchorman announced "Several long range missiles have just hit the general area of Tel Aviv. Our experts believe they where fired by Hezbollah from south Lebanon."

"Oy vey," blurted Ganot. "Another war coming with Hezbollah. We didn't do that well last time."

"Not to worry, Zalman," assured Inbar, forking a piece of grilled fish into his mouth. "In 2006 we didn't have a Prime Minister with land warfare at his fingertips."

*

"Zelzal-2 Iranian-built missiles fitted with 600 kilogram high-explosive warheads," conveyed the Israel Defense Forces (IDF) Chief of Staff at a special emergency meeting of the security cabinet in Jerusalem.

"That's the retaliation we expected for our airborne attack on Iran," Prime Minister Sharon stated. "We need to ensure they don't impede bigger operations coming shortly."

"I say we just take out their missiles from the air," the IAF commander proposed.

"Nah," said Sharon. "Forget surgical strikes. That didn't work too well in 2006. Then and now, what would lick these turban heads is a several division sized assault along the entire border, coupled with maritime and air attacks."

"That risks bringing Syria into a full scale confrontation with our forces, Ariel," warned the Defense Minister.

"Bashar Al Assad is no longer in control there. The new government isn't that tightly allied with Iran. We'll take the risk."

"It's a go, then?" asked the Chief of Staff.

"Not yet Lieutenant General. Maybe this won't be needed after all. There are always unimagined turns, especially in our mad region. Prepare to begin the operation on shortest notice and hold. Anything else?"

"We must also immediately retaliate for today's attack," reminded the Minister of Defense.

"Of course, " Sharon turned to the Head of Mossad, responsible for covert operations. "Activate Silent Rooster, kill that big mouth."

"We'll do our best, Arik. Hard to get to him, always hiding in deep bunkers."

Sharon glanced at the tense faces around him, then smiled and suggested, "Enjoy the rest of your Passover, everyone. I'm going back to sleep. A little more tired at 85 than I used to be. "

*

Two days later a Lebanese Druze working for Mossad who was spying on Hezbollah and its Iranian Revolutionary Guard advisors provided intelligence that a substantial number of high officials of the Shi'a organization, including its Secretary General, were going to attend a meeting in Tehran. A team of eight Mossad agents travelling on bogus passports then arrived in Tehran to prepare the assassination of Hezbollah's Secretary General.

33

A fisherman standing on a floating wooden structure cast his line into the oily surface of Baku's bay. Off in the distance he could see other fishermen standing by their lines along the rocky shore in old, inoperative oil fields. He heard a strong rumbling sound, looked up the shore and watched a large southbound fishing boat careening with the strong west-northerly wind on white capped waves.

The fisherman didn't know that the forty five meter long decked trawler was carrying 30 US Navy Seals outfitted on a mission to destroy the implosion devices in Parchin. They have boarded dressed as fishermen at Azerbaijan's capital city of Baku carrying the latest in personal high-tech weapons and gadgets. Several FAVs were also hauled. Now they were heading to the southern coast of the Caspian, largest enclosed body of water in the world, a hybrid between a lake and a sea fed by many rivers including the mighty Volga.

At the Combat Information Center (CIC) an officer muttered, "Would you believe these tough guys can actually get sea sick? Look at those two vomiting their lunch into the murky water there."

The superior CIC officer said, "Best way to get this job done, though. High command is still traumatized with the fiasco of Eagle Claw."

"That was so many years ago. Couldn't we destroy the damn thing from the air?"

"Guess not. Probably dug too deep underground. This may be the only workable alternative to a direct nuclear strike. We're not there yet. Is that a tough call for you?"

"Check these German Shepherds throwing up at the fish hold below the working deck. What are they for?"

"Bomb sniffing. They also provide additional night vision with the infrared cameras that will be attached to their bodies once they get on combat ground. Now keep your snoopy eyes on the monitor and shut up."

34

The sea was calm on the next morning and the trawler was advancing southbound at a speed of 8 knots, having gone much slower most of the stormy night. The special unit's leader standing on the bow still couldn't see land ahead when he was warned by the CIC officer that a large Iranian patrol boat was whizzing toward him from the resort town of Bablosar on the south shore. "They locked you on their radar. Prepare to take them out," an order descended from the command center. He walked to the bridge, called one of the unit's several Farsi speaking Seals to stay with him and the others to stay out of sight inside the accommodation cabins at the lower deck. When the patrol boat came within his view on the left side he ordered three other Seals to put on their combat diving outfit and lay aft. Fifteen minutes later the Iranian boat was rumbling close at the trawler's port side. A loudspeaker carried speech in Farsi. "They want to board us to check if we've caught Sturgeon," the Seal on the bridge said. "Fishing them for caviar is forbidden now."

"Drop your Seals to blow the patrol boat," the CIC officer ordered. But the Seal held his leader's shoulder, picked the bridge's loudspeaker and began conversing with the Iranian loudspeaker. "What the hell are you doing, soldier?" the CIC yelled. "Proceed to kill as ordered." Nothing of the sort happened. Instead the Farsi conversation continued for several long minutes. The patrol boat then revved its engine and took off back to the Iranian shore.

"How'd you do that?" marveled the Seal leader.

"Easy, I know my people."

"Details," shouted the CIC back in the United States.

"No need to get into that. In view of the big amounts of money involved with Beluga caviar, enforcers of the prohibition to fish Sturgeon are known to turn a blind eye."

"Great, I was about to order a drone attack. You saved us that."

"Right, beats the hustle of a naval battle or drones. But it's still going to cost the US taxpayer a lot of cash."

*

Around midnight the trawler reached the insertion point on a relatively isolated stretch of sand beach just east of Khesht Sar. The commandos changed to their high-tech garb including video cameras on their helmets. They outfitted their dogs with ballistic body armor to protect them from bullets and shrapnel, hauled their FAVs to the shore, disembarked into the vehicles and within minutes drove off in long distance travel formation onto a small southbound path.

35

The FAVs carrying the Navy Seals traveled southbound in cultivated farmland and lush forests. At dead of night they came to a traffic circle northwest of the town of Parchin, turned right on the first exit and stopped several hundred yards south of the circle. They attached the infrared cameras to the dogs and brought down the sentries at the base's watchtowers with long range .50 caliber sniper rifles. They then assaulted the military base in frontal attack formation. Most soldiers at the base were sleeping in their barracks. The FAVs split, each vehicle stopping at the entrance of a dormitory structure. Two navy Seals entered each of these and aimed their automatic rifles at the Iranians in their beds. At the same time, two FAVs carrying eight commandos and two bomb sniffing dogs stopped at the bunker that Israeli and US analysts believed led to an underground hideout of the implosion devices. All this action was followed by the President and key members of the cabinet back at the Situation Room in the White House.

The dogs jumped out and sniffed around the structure, followed by their trainers holding the leashes. They walked all around it but couldn't find an opening.

One of the dogs then stopped cold before the bare wall of the bunker. Examining it closely, the Seals saw a small cavity. Their leader pushed it and a whitewashed plastic cover opened sideways, revealing two rectangular metal devices with glass surfaces. "Fingerprint and Iris identification, " a CIC technician monitoring the operation conveyed. The commando leader barked a short order. Within minutes the Iranian commanding officer of the base was brought to the structure. He was forced at gunpoint to lay his thumb on the fingerprint biometric device and stare into the Iris recognition device. To the right of the biometrics, a sliding panel then opened.

36

The Seals leader and four of his men advanced cautiously in urban combat mode through the bunker's doorway, leaving the three other Seals with the Iranian officer keeping guard outside. They shined their flashlights, saw stairs and watchfully descended three flights to a long corridor. They proceeded for three minutes along the corridor, arriving at a platform with several compartments. "Mine shaft," a CIC expert said. "The largest compartment is a mine cage." The Seals entered the large double-decked cage, which basically functioned like an elevator. The leader pushed in a button bearing a down arrow symbol. The cage then made a vertical descent of about 800 yards, reaching the floor of a medium sized cave. The Seals stepped into the cave and shined their flashlights around. "There," said the leader, indicating a vault door at the opposite wall of the cave. He walked over to the bank style door and examined it under his flashlight. It had a key change combination lock protected with seven massive metal cylinders extending from the door into the frame. He took out a sophisticated penetrating device from his backpack and applied it on the lock, revealing the internal mechanism. A CIC expert activated specialized software to

122

deduce the combination. Less than a minute later the leader placed his left hand on the combination lock and manipulated it in the sequence indicated by the expert. He pulled on the handle and the door turned with micron-range precision on its roller-thrust bearing hinges.

The Seal leader stepped around the door and turned his flashlight around into a small bunker-like space. "Steel-reinforced concrete," a CIC vault expert said. There was nothing in it but two small metal crates lying on the floor in the middle. The leader centered the light on them. "The pits must be inside these crates," a CIC nuclear expert advised. The Seal leader knew the expert was talking about the cores of the implosion devices. "Take the crates and let's get the hell out of here," he rapped.

37

"Tell me Josiah," requested Rona Inbar. "What's your take on the 'secret' that the Ein Gedi synagogue inscription warns the people not to reveal?" They were sitting together with Daniela and Michael Inbar around a coffee table at Michael's apartment in Jerusalem.

"It must be referring to the Halfis living there. Yoseh bar Halfi resided in Ein Gedi before he moved to Jerusalem. But he's left his family in Ein Gedi. Ya'acov bar Halfi lived in nearby Qumran."

"You seem to take great interest in that family name," remarked Daniela. "I remember your comments about that tax collector in Capernaum. I also noticed the Halfi name inscribed somewhere at the synagogue there."

"Same family," he stated.

"But the synagogue inscriptions at both Capernaum and Ein Gedi are much later than first century A.D., Josiah."

"I know Rona. Back then people used to pass names for generations."

"Why would that name be such a terrible secret, Josiah?" asked Daniela.

"Because they were afraid of the Romans."

"Assuming that's indeed the same family mentioned in the New Testament, they would certainly be afraid," opined Rona. "The Romans were searching for and executing each person rumored to be a descendant of King David… anyone who the people may follow as a Messiah come to lead an armed revolt against them. In fact, two grandsons of Jesus' brother Judah have been first tried and released by Roman Emperor Domitian in the 90s A.D., then tried again and put to death by Emperor Trajan a few years later."

"They executed Judah's grandsons? This is the first time I hear about that," he reacted sadly.

38

Half an hour after the Seals began the assault of
Parchin they were distancing rapidly southbound from it on
the Iranian high plateau. After they'd traveled about 70
miles, most of that in total desolation, they reached a sea of
sand, spotted with flat white tracks of dry hard packed salt.
In the darkness surrounding them the bizarre scenery
seemed even more surrealistic through their night vision
goggles. That was part of the Dasht e Kavir, or Great Salt
Desert. The meeting point with recovery helicopters.

The Navy Seals descended from their FAVs, trying
to locate the helicopters. Not one was there. Unknown to
the Special Forces unit, the helicopters flew in under radar
into a cloud of fine sand particles suspended in the air,
known as Haboob, and aborted their mission. The Seals
radioed their base and were told helicopters would take off
again for them as soon as the unexpected weather
phenomenon clears. But if that doesn't happen within an
hour, the commandos would have to hold for the following
night.

The hour having passed with the Haboob still in the
air, the Seals camouflaged the FAVs and hid as best they
could in the open plain. The leader ordered two Seals to
take lookout positions at a silent highway about a mile to
their west. The day came and passed without a single soul

disturbing them. Then the radio crackled that five stealth Blackhawk helicopters have taken off for the commandos. The modified version of these choppers allowed the tail rotor to spin more slowly, reducing the loud whirring that helicopters usually make. Other changes to the helicopter included special radar absorbing material and gentler curved angles to reduce radar detection. The Seals' leader was therefore confident the Blackhawks should be able to make the extraction without further incident. But before two hours passed he was rocked by a huge explosion coming from the highway's direction as a southbound tanker truck was blown up there by an anti-tank shoulder missile.

"What the hell happened," the Seals' leader hollered into his throat microphone.

"The truck's headlight beams hit on us. The driver took out the CB. He might have spotted us."

"Stay put there. Hopefully he hasn't alerted anyone," commanded the leader. *Prepare for the worst now*, he thought.

But a few minutes later they heard the familiar chopping sound of helicopters. The Blackhawks were less than one hundred yards away. Within moments the pilots landed them on the nearest salt patch, actually aided by the ample lighting from the blazing truck.

PART THREE

A Doomsday Scenario

39

In Tehran, senior commanders of the military establishment were meeting with colleagues from Hezbollah and Hamas to coordinate a plan for combined attack of Israel. The Iranian military chief summed the plan up.

"Hezbollah and Hamas will simultaneously fire missiles of all ranges, rockets and mortars at the Zionist entity's cities, towns, bases, military installations and airports. If we get the Syrians on board, they will also fire missiles with chemical and biological warheads. After ten days of that bombardment we'll begin the land operation. Syrian tank divisions reinforced by several of our IRG armored brigades will advance in four attack columns to take the Golan Heights with massive air and artillery support. Concurrently Hezbollah reinforced with IRG mobile units will penetrate the Upper Galilee. During the entire operation Hezbollah will continue to fire missiles at targets in the Lower Galilee, Haifa, Nathania and Tel Aviv. Hamas will fire missiles at Ashdod, Beer Sheba, Ashkelon and other targets in the south of the country."

"When do we start?"

"Our President will coordinate the simultaneous combined assault with the leaders of Syria, Hamas and Hezbollah after completion of the operational preparation.

Before that, we want a gradual escalation. Hezbollah will commence controlled firing of rockets and missiles A.S.A.P."

*

At a small general aviation airport serving Tehran that was secured heavily by Iranian Revolutionary Guards, a woman cleaning a Learjet's lavatory switched a metal ashtray with an identical looking ashtray from her cleaning tool basket. It was a sophisticated, fast reaction rate powerful explosive device made entirely from metal and oxides of metal. The woman continued cleaning the business jet for twelve minutes then descended its staircase just when Hezbollah participants of the strategic meeting arrived at the airport. Twenty minutes later the Learjet took off for Beirut. When it reached altitude of 8000 feet, it exploded into little pieces in the sky. An hour later the Head of Mossad informed Prime Minister Sharon that Hezbollah's Secretary General had been eliminated.

40

The chilly rain drizzling over the humid summer tropical river was creating a rainbow in the sky. The birds chirping and the sound of the nearby river were truly tranquil. A beautiful Tukan bird rested on an extended tree branch that hung over the river. The river, which came down the valley in a spectacular series of waterfalls, had a little red school of fish swimming near its surface; they were visible to the Tukan. The bird took off and flew in the river's downward path. The red fish swam down the river into the great lake. They went lower into the depths of the murky water. All the fish were greenish blue now. They were all deep underwater where the red light could not reach them.

Rona opened her eyes and stared at the paramedics inside the ambulance, then closed them again.

The fish came to a great sunken ship, entering it through the many cracks in the hull. Inside the ship blew a horn-like sound. The hull broke and the water rushed in. It moved quickly inside the sunken ship and gushed most of the fish out. When the water's movement stopped a new noise became audible. The fish scattered.

Rona opened her eyes in a blue and green room filled with doctors, nurses, sterile surgical steel utensils and several injured men and women. A man lying next to her was severely burned. His lips were all cut up, his face swollen to third degree burns, his eyes useless. Two voluted patches of bloody puffy skin, like little black derby, were stuck to where the center of his left eye would have been. His right cheek was almost completely gone revealing two of his upper molars and part of his high cheek bones.

Back in Jerusalem Michael Inbar was informed by telephone that his wife had been injured during a rocket attack on Haifa, where she went that morning to visit a high school friend. Michael drove his car madly to the hospital in Haifa. But when he got there a nurse told him Rona had just died.

41

Before Michael was back in Jerusalem on that day, the IAF attacked Hezbollah's munitions depots, missile and rocket fixed and mobile launch installations, command centers and strongholds all over Lebanon. On the next day the Israel Defense Forces (IDF) began a massive broad ground assault into Lebanon with several armored and infantry divisions. Israel's navy imposed a total maritime blockade on Lebanon, blowing up bridges, roads and other means of transport into the battle zone south of the capital Beirut. The IAF began bombing Lebanese infrastructure. Paratrooper units landed north of the Litany river, blocking all southbound and northbound traffic, effectively cutting Lebanon in two.

Hezbollah still managed to hit Israel's civilian population, especially in the center of the country. While many projectiles were hit mid-air by Israel's Iron Dome defense system, and many rockets and missiles harmlessly fell in empty spaces, some reached their targets. Scores of medium and long range missiles hit each of the towns Ramat-Gan, Kfar Saba, Nathania and the city of Tel Aviv causing dozens of dead and hundreds of wounded there. At the same time Hamas fired many medium and short range missiles on cities and towns in the southern region of Israel, which suffered lower casualties than the center. But everything remained quiet at the Syrian border. No ground attack or missiles materialized from there. The new Syrian government apparently worried more about its shaky control in Damascus than about Iran's jihadist ambitions and wisely avoided a belligerent clash with Israel.

Within three days after the Israeli assault began, the missile rain over its civilians began to fizzle. Two days later the Israelis crossed the Litany, pushing Hezbollah fighters far enough north to protect Israel against the few missiles still in Hezbollah's arsenal. The fighters south of the Litany were hit first in their tunnels with bunker busting clever bombs from IAF aircraft then hunted down by IDF infantry. Most of these fighters were killed and the rest were captured, disarmed and taken to POW camps inside Israel, on southbound convoys packed with victorious Israeli soldiers chanting "Arik King of Israel" for their old warrior Prime Minister.

42

"Is immediate danger from Iran over now?" enquired the President at the White House, during the next regular meeting of her national security cabinet.

"I'm afraid not, Madam," the Director of National Intelligence advised. "We believe they had enough material for production of four to five implosion devices. Our Navy Seals took two of these…at this time we don't know where they are."

"Hmm, so they can still fit these devices as warheads on long range missiles," She turned to the National Security Adviser, "What's your take?"

"Maintain NORAD on high alert. Instruct STRATCOM to coordinate a preemptive tactical nuclear strike with our command units in the Persian Gulf and the Diego Garcia military base."

"Maintain NORAD, prepare STRATCOM, gentlemen. The chance we'd have to use nukes there is infinitely small, but we must always be ready for unknown variables."

In layman's terms, NORAD is the North American Aerospace Defense Command that controls the Early Warning System (EWS). The system was designed to warn of an impending nuclear attack and provide the United States the capability to launch on these warnings. USSTRATCOM is U.S. Strategic Command.

43

Rona Inbar was buried during the brief war. When
her body was lowered to the grave Michael howled in
agony "will our wars never end?"

Josiah ben David then stood over the grave, and
proclaimed "There shall come from the sky a certain
exalted man who spreads his hands on the many-fruited
tree, the noblest of Hebrews, who one day caused the sun to
stand still, when he cried with fair speech and pure lips.

Then the well-springs of wickedness will close off, evil
will be banished by righteousness as darkness is banished
before light, and as smoke ceases to be, evil will forever end
and righteousness will be revealed as is the sun that holds
fast the world. And all those who believe in the secrets of
Belial will be no more. Knowledge shall fill the earth and
perversion will cease.

Day and night meditate on the approaching
mystery and study it always. Then you will know truth and
injustice, wisdom and folly in all their ways. Then you will

know the difference between good and evil relating to their deeds. For the God of knowledge is the foundation of truth, and through the approaching mystery He set apart its foundation, the work of His hands. And in pure understanding were revealed the secrets of His thought with the perfect conduct in all his deeds. Always seek those eagerly, and understand all their results. And then you will know everlasting glory and His marvelous mysteries, and the might of His deeds. And you will understand the beginning of your reward at the memorial of the time that has come. Engraved is the decree and all the visitation is determined. For God's ordinance is engraved over all the iniquities, and a book of memorial is written before Him for those who keep His word."

Is he ever going to stop tormenting me with this religious drivel, ruminated Inbar.

44

Back in his office eight days after Rona's funeral Inbar handed his secretary two sealed plastic envelopes. One envelope held a pen that Josiah ben David had used at Inbar's apartment and the other envelope contained a strand of the young man's hair. "Dispatch these to forensics at Mount Scopus," he instructed. "The pen for fingerprints and the hair for DNA identification."

Inbar then called two of his deputies to his office, shut the door and instructed them to see to bugging the young man's apartment. Use state of the art surveillance on his cell phone, track his emails and put a 24:7 tail on him.

"What about the legality of all this, Michael?" worried one of the deputies.

"Yeah. Of course. Dig up all court orders for these operations, where necessary by law. I want the transcripts of all recordings of any and all his chats and conversations brought to my office. I want to see them every morning on my desk here, along with a full report of anyone he met or spoke with in person, on the phone or by email, where and when."

Two days later the forensic lab reported no identification on comparison of the fingerprints and DNA to police databases. But a superintendent at the Biology Department wanted to discuss the DNA findings with Inbar. He told his secretary to set up the meeting. An hour later he boarded his clunker at the parking lot of the police district headquarters in central Jerusalem and took ten minutes to drive to the sprawling complex of the national police headquarters at Mount Scopus, overlooking a full panorama of the old city of Jerusalem, the Temple Mount and the gold domed Mosque in its center splendidly arrayed, the Mount of Olives to the left.

45

"The DNA we've extracted from the hair you've provided is extremely interesting," the superintendent said in her office at the Division of Forensic Identification Unit of the Israel Police. "Can you tell me who it comes from, Inspector Inbar?"

"A young man living here in Jerusalem."

"How old?"

"30."

"Tell me everything you know about his background."

"Other than his date of birth, nothing. That's actually the reason I sent you the fingerprints and hair."

"I see. Do you know his ethnicity?"

"Nope. As I said, nothing at all. It's actually as if he's never existed. What's special about his DNA?"

"It's identical to ancient Judean DNA."

"What's unusual about that in Jewish men? We all originate from this country." After over 1100 years of national history in the Land of Israel, Jews dispersed throughout the world. Michael knew that many DNA tests were conducted to reconstruct the geographical origins of Jewish populations of the various Diaspora communities and that they all originated from a common place that must be their ancient homeland. Rona had once cited a conclusion of an expert from the US National Academy of Science *'Despite their long-term residence in different countries and isolation from one another, most Jewish populations were not significantly different from one another at the genetic level.'*

"While the main ethnic origin of Ashkenazim is ancient Israelite, they also evidence discordance from European peoples from the northern Mediterranean region, Slavs and Khazars. The main genetic element of Sephardim is also Israelite, but they have small influence from various other people. Jews from North Africa are mainly Israelite but show small traces of Berber infusion. Georgian, Yemenite and Cochin Jews of India are a mix of host populations and Israelites. Ethiopian Jews have little or no Israelite ancestry."

"The point being?"

"We've tested the subject Y-DNA to determine the origin of the man's paternal line. That test strictly checks the male descendency line, with no maternal genetic input. We've also tested his Mitochondrial DNA for his maternal descendency," she paused.

Inbar knew these tests can provide evidence of ancient origin. "Continue," he requested.

"Both DNAs contain no foreign genetic element. Nothing at all. .signature. That man cannot possibly exist here and now."

46

In Pentecost, Daniela and Josiah hiked around Jerusalem's Mount of Olives. When they reached the southern slope of the ridge he stopped, focusing downhill. "What do you see, Josiah?" she asked. "There used to be a village there, called 'Beit Anya.' Reminds me of a passage in a book I've read describing the bethroding ceremony of Judah's Royals in biblical times. It's a ceremony occurring during this feast of Shavuot. Here goes," he recited:

"The Prince was carried on a throne, surrounded by scores of Judah's best soldiers wearing swords. The throne was made of cedars of Lebanon. Its posts were silver, the back was gold, and the seat was covered with purple cloth. With the prince came the sweet smell of spices, of myrrh and frankincense.

And the seventeen-year-old prince sang to his bride, 'My darling. You are lovely, so very lovely. As you look through your veil, your eyes are those of a dove. Your hair tosses about gracefully. Your teeth are white and match perfectly. Your lips are crimson cords. Your mouth is shapely and your temple as pomegranate under your braids. Your neck is built upright as the tower of David, decorated with thousands of warriors' shields. Your breasts like twin deer feeding on roses. I will hasten to those twin hills sprinkled with myrrh and frankincense and stay till sunrise.'

The fifteen-year-old bride answered singing, 'Let the north wind blow, the south wind too. Let them spread the aroma of my garden, so the one I love may enter and taste its delicious fruit.'

Off they were carried to the bridal chamber in the palace, while he sang, 'My bride, my very own. I come to my garden and enjoy its spices. I eat my honeycomb and honey. I drink my wine and milk'."

"I have one question to you, Josiah, and I want you to tell me the truth," Daniela delivered gravely. "Who are you?"

Josiah sat down on a rock facing west, took in the sight of the Temple Mount across the Kidron creek. Late butterflies were tasting the budding Roses of Sharon flowers in the precipitous Kidron Valley below the City of David excavations. Olive trees were growing there, Josiah sighed and invited Daniela, "Sit here beside me and I'll tell you what I know."

47

"I grew up in a small town in Italy, called Assisi, " Josiah spoke dreamily. "I don't of course remember my infancy, but I always had foggy visions and impressions that couldn't be, yet felt real. Of limpid mountain air carrying in the smells and distant sounds of evenings. Of sheep speckling valleys and limestone hills surrounding me... of dogs barking and of camels belching...

Other pictures come of rock-cobbled streets flanked by terraced houses yellow with age... Of a wedding procession moving down a street, a band of hired musicians at the front extolling the couple and the bliss that awaits them... Small wooden carts laden with wedding presents drawn by a donkey at the end of the procession... Everyone in the procession singing fervently in honor of the bride and groom. The men clapping their hands and the women dancing sinuously to the rhythm...

Another impression of dinners served by house servants in bowls to about ten people that I feel are members of two related families... Some of the bowls with flat bases, shallow profiles and straight, cut rims; others deep. The inner surface is red in color and burnished with concentric rings... The men and women are eating lamb meat and semolina mixed in olive oil...drinking diluted wine poured from decanters... This is often followed by a sensation of strolling in an orchard...The orchard is filled with pomegranate, fig and olive trees within ripe vines and waters rippling nearby...

Other pictures of a man directing a plow and pushing its handle down... I am directing oxen pulling the plow by a yoke made of wood and placed on the back of the their necks with ropes... A young man proceeding behind me is holding a seed bag on his shoulder and dropping the seeds into a funnel... The seeds are falling to the ground through the pipe, emerging behind the plow point...

Other pictures of a field of barley... Reapers led by a foreman advancing slowly, their bodies gleaming with sweat... They seize a bunch of stalks with one hand, while reaping it with sickles held by the other hand... joyous maidens and young men coming behind the reapers... The maidens collecting the harvested stalks left lying on the ground by the reapers into the bosoms of their garments... The young men following them bounding the bunches of stalks into sheaves and putting them in piles.... The poor coming behind all workers.. they are gleaning the ears of the stalks...

Now visions of wagons, animals and people carrying large baskets of harvested stalks... Workers by night separating barley grains from the stalks on a platform made of three wooden boards... The front of the board is upturned. The bottom of the platform is embedded with hard flint stones... The workers are throwing material into the air with forks... The forks are made of wood and have many prongs... the wind separated the mixture... the grain, it falls down first... next the small pieces of straw fall down in a different place... then the chaff falls down farthest.... Now other workers using wooden shovels are collecting the grain into heaps...

Wadi cliffs in a wilderness... crevices... a cave...high above the wadi floor...I am contemplating scrolls...

A river... People in torn clothes... Some laughing aloud... Some talking to themselves... Some repeatedly and incessantly shouting... Some making fists toward the sky... Some making obscene gestures and muttering incoherently... All moving slowly as if in a dream... One man with eyes blazing and saliva rolling over his beard... I am energetic and agitated, munching my teeth... I am standing up trembling with closed eyes... I am stretching my body to the sky... I am waving my arms in the air... I am walking back the way I came... I am running... I am falling to the ground... I am breathing regularly....

A caravan of camels advancing slowly in the last rays of the setting sun...

Hot wind raising dust...

Servants wiping dining tables at roadway inns...

Fishermen rowing boats on placid water... Lanterns at the edges of the fishing boats... Fresh fish sold in markets...

Visions of lush vineyards planted in terraces... They are surrounded by fences and contain watchtowers... Some are enclosed with stone walls...

Drinking wine in taverns... bawdy faces of men and women around me...

Impressions of entering a city through a monumental gate... A rectangular structure comprising several guard chambers and gateways... The facade has a projecting tower... The central passage is about four meters in width... A casemate wall flanks the gate... The city is standing along a mountain road, among fruit trees planted on terraces, buttressed by stones...

Visions of little shops along a main street bazaar steaming with haggling fervor of shopkeepers and housewives... Porters carrying complete forelegs of beef across a wet city plaza... They go into a butcher shop bordering a corner... Many ships moored by the seashore along the street... Shops are plentiful with elegant bowls and cups, red-and-cream polished tableware, elegant decorated wine pitchers and drinking cups.... Sailors drunk roaming the streets.... A woman on the roof of one of the buildings offering frankincense in a small incense altar made of sandstone.... A flutist leading a procession of women singing... The women carry around a half meter long puppet with a penis almost as large... They are operating this penis up and down with strings ...They are all swaggering on their feet...

Another picture... hundreds of officers... They are overseeing thousands of forced laborers... Working on a huge construction project...

A vision of women dancing and swinging timbrels, other women ringing on metal triangles and men striking cymbals and playing flutes in a procession...exalted crowds cheering along the route... many are singing in voices of gladness...

Now a ceremony of some sort in a large hall...visions of two men dressed in long silken robes standing at the far short side of the hall blowing long and slender and perfectly straight clarions widening gradually in front into bell mouths... The air blowing from these clarions fashioned from silver flutters in D Minor arpeggios... Musicians standing opposite the two men begin to sing... Male voices on the left side and female voices sung in falsetto by men on the right... The musicians start to play various instruments whose strings are drawn across sandalwood... They are plucking harps of ten strings and of six strings in soprano... Lyres of symmetrical and asymmetrical types are being struck and pulled an octave higher than the clarions... The singers are bowing their heads and start singing solemnly in slow time without a distinct rhythm or melodious cadence, in recited music... Cymbals are struck several times during the singing... the music on the whole coming out in unison...A man stands stiffly erect under heavy ceremonial clothes by an altar at the far end of the hall... He is shining with precious stones... an apron is encircling his body from the loins downward... His garment is rounded in shape... It looks like gold in blue, purple and crimson material... The man is wearing a breast piece on the shoulder pieces of the garment... It looks like a cross between a square plate and a hollow pouch... Many precious stones are fixed into that breastplate… The garment includes three pairs of rings, two chains and two frames, all of them gold,… Two lapis-lazuli stones also adorn the shoulder pieces of the ceremonial robe… Golden bells are also attached to its skirts… A pomegranate is suspended between each bell…The man wears a golden diadem on his head…

A sensation of soldiers shoving me into a pillared court… They are setting me to a hall… A man is seated majestically on a pedestal in the hall… He is examining me… I am immersed in anguish and frustration…

Walking within poppies dancing in fields… Gilded meadows meeting domes of black rocks… Gnarled olive trees… Hills covered with boulders of black basalt… Symphony of blazing colors… A lake… Deep blue waters… Ground rising steeply in fertile green… Houses made of basalt stones… Snow covered peak in the distance…

*

"The town of Assisi where I grew up lies sixty kilometers north of Rome. It is mostly famous as the birthplace of Saint Francis. I was raised in a Catholic seminary at a villa there. After I graduated high school I was sent to a college where I received classical and religious education. This consisted of meditations, conferences, recitations of scripture and frequent consultations with my spiritual director. Every weekday I rose up at five in the morning, made my meditation for half an hour, heard Mass and usually received Communion. On Sundays I assisted at solemn High Mass and at Vespers. After six years of this training I was ordained as a Catholic priest. But when the Second Lebanon War between Israel and Hezbollah broke out in July of 2006, I felt an unstoppable urge to come to this country. I changed my name and here I am."

"What about your parents, Josiah?"

"I never knew who they were. I was told that a woman brought me over to the seminary when I was a toddler. Never found out who that woman was."

"What's your Italian name?"

"Salvatore de Luca."

48

"I'm going out of the country for a few days," said Inbar on the next evening at his apartment." Is that okay with you?"

"Where to?"

"Rome."

"Take me with you, Dad."

"You have school Jonathan."

"I can't listen to anything at school now."

"I guess Mom would have wanted me to take you. Come along then."

*

After they cleared customs and immigration at Fumicino airport, Michael and Jonathan Inbar exited to the passenger arrival taxi line. Jonathan said, "Let's just take this one," looking at an irregular, unmarked taxi.

"Nah," said Michael. "Let's go into the next legal one."

"Same thing, just cheaper."

"Get into the good taxi and I'll tell you why."

They entered the taxi, Jonathan next to the driver and his father in the rear seat. Jonathan said, "To the Rome Hilton, please."

The driver pushed the meter on and took off.

"What was that about, Dad?"

"Once I came here with Mom around midnight on Alitalia from Tel Aviv. One of these improperly working drivers offered to take us to Rome for less than the regular licensed taxis. We took it and he began driving. Mom started talking to him in Italian. I asked her what was said and she told me the driver quoted 90,000 lire for the run. I said 'Tell him no way, Rona. It only costs 25,000 lire, but they always say they have to charge twice for the way back to the airport. Never heard any driver ask for 90,000 lire. '

Mom turned and started a more heated confabulation with the man.

'What is the bandit saying now, Rona?' I asked.

'He says damn us. He could have taken an American who doesn't know his way around here. Instead he had to take Italian speaking Jews. Should I tell him to drive us back to the taxi line?'

I laughed, 'Nah. Tell him to drive us to Rome and I'll give 35,000 lire.' But when we got there I gave him 60,000 lire for the fun."

"What did he do, then?"

"Cursed 'vaffanculo' and drove off."

49

On the next morning Michael and Jonathan went to the Vatican. They stood in line to enter Saint Peter's Basilica. But when they reached the head of the line a policeman refused to let Jonathan proceed, because he was wearing shorts. "Disrespectful," he said. So they went over to the wall flanking the complex, stood in another line to enter the Capella Sistina and saw that. Next they walked the streets to the Pantheon. Coming out they saw a stylized gelato shop across the Plaza and went to chose some from innumerable delicious flavors. Sitting in the teaming street outside the shop, Michael said, "Now we have to go rent a car. I want to drive to a place called Assisi tomorrow."

"What's there to see?"

"A lot of churches and such. I have some investigation to do there."

"Why's that?"

"Turns out Daniela's friend Josiah grew up there, at some sort of convent."

"What's that to you, Dad?"

"Some strange things always happen around him."

"Yeah. He's not a criminal, though."

"But we do have to go to Assisi. Long story."

"But I haven't seen Saint Peter's Cathedral yet. You go to Assisi tomorrow and I'll stay here in Rome."

On the next morning Inbar rose up quietly, dressed up, existed the hotel room on tip toes, leaving Jonathan asleep, descended to the parking, started a rented white Alfa Romeo and drove into an Italian sunrise.

*

About an hour and a half later Inbar reached Assisi, located on a slope of Monte Subasio in central Italy and renowned as the birthplace of St. Francis, the founder of the Franciscan order. He drove by the signs to a church and monastery called San Damiano. A priest came over to him greeting, "Buongiorno."

"Good morning, Father. My name is Michael Inbar. I'm from Israel."

"Good morning, Sir," the priest returned. "What brings you here at this time of morning?"

"I'm looking for some information about a seminary student called Salvatore de Luca."

"I'm Padre Roberto Sciavoni, head of this seminary of Saint Damiano. I remember Salvatore well. I hear he lives in Jerusalem now. How's he doing?"

"Real well. He's a close friend of my daughter's."

"Oh. I understand. Father's interest in daughter's future spouse?"

"Something like that, Padre."

"Salvatore studied here for about six years. Remarkable young man. Magnetic presence. Always speaks in hyperbole. I'd never heard anyone say anything bad about him. And that's a rarity, if you know what I mean."

"Where did he pass his childhood, Padre?"

"On the grounds of the attached monastery here."

"Where was he born?"

"You baffle me, Mr. Inbar. You should ask him yourself."

"He doesn't know."

155

Jonathan was walking slowly along the walls of Saint Peter's Basilica at the Vatican, admiring the late renaissance architecture, artwork and statues, notably those by Michelangelo.

A uniformed official came up to Jonathan. *God...* he thought. *Not the dress code again.* But the official had no beef with the teenager. "Good morning sir," he greeted Jonathan. "Would you mind following me?"

The official went through magnificent corridors to a sumptuous office. A red robed clergyman came forward saying, "Good morning, young man. My name is Cardinal Giuseppe Chiaro. I'm the Secretary of State of the Vatican. And this is my assistant Antonio Belli." He introduced a younger clergyman. "Please sit down," the Cardinal indicated a sofa. "Did you have breakfast yet?"

"Thanks but no thanks," Jonathan blurted. "What gets me the honors?"

"We understand you know a person we have great interest in."

"Don't tell me, Josiah ben David?"

"He did choose a remarkable name."

"My father is here to snoop some about him, too."

"We know that. How is Salvatore doing?"

"Josiah? He's a sort of superman. In a spiritual way. My half brother Avi is another sort of superman. In a physical way. His friends say he has ice in his blood. I find they complete each other like two gloves. Merged together they'd be Top God."

"Where was Salvatore's kindergarten, Padre?' inquired Inbar. "Do you know?"

"Not off hand, sir. Of course we keep records of all children who grew up within the premises of the monastery. Please wait here for a moment." He went over to a black line phone where he conversed for several minutes in Italian. He then returned and said "Salvatore attended our kindergarten here."

"Can I go to the office, Padre?"

"What for?"

"Well, maybe they have personal records of him."

"You're a pro, aren't you sir? I begin wondering about your cover story."

Inbar produced a family photo, indicating, "Here's Salvatore, sitting between my daughter Daniela and her mother Leora. I am standing behind them."

"I see. He looks happy. The kindergarten is in the garden outside the Church building. The teacher or one of her assistants will show you into the office. Good luck."

*

"We don't have records of anything unusual happening with Salvatore," the fortyish woman at the kindergarten office put forth.

"Do you have pictures of the class of 1986?"

She took out an album and showed Inbar a picture. "That's the only one I have, sir."

"This must be the teacher back then, right?" He indicated the only adult in the picture. "Can you give me her name and address?"

She checked on the office computer and scribbled a note. "Here, sir," she amiably delivered. Inbar returned to the Alfa at the parking area of the Church and tried to call Jonathan on his cellphone. Jonathan's cellphone returned, "Customer out of reach." Inbar entered the address scribbled on the note into his navigation GPS and drove off.

*

A fifty something woman opened her apartment door, saying something in Italian. "Do you speak English, Signora?" he bid.

"I do. How can I help you?"

"I was referred to you from the kindergarten at San Damiano," he produced the note.

"Come in." She showed him into the apartment and they sat on couches in the living room, facing each other over a small coffee table. He accepted her offer for coffee and she stepped into her kitchen to make it.

"What did you want to see me for?" she asked, returning with two cups. He sipped of the coffee while repeating the introduction previously given to the priest.

"I loved little Salvatore," she smiled broadly. "All his schoolmates adored him."

"He says he was told a woman had brought him to the monastery. Do you know who she was?"

158

"I'm not sure if she's the same one, but there was a woman who'd made several visits to see him for a few months of his first year. Let me check." She stood up and went to her bedroom. Several minutes later she emerged with a picture album. "That's her, " she indicated a woman hugging a toddler blowing at a birthday cake with three lit candles.

"Do you know her name?" Inbar asked.

"I can't remember after so many years... but wait, I'm pretty sure..." She took the picture out of the album and flipped to the backside.

"You're lucky, I have her full name and address here. I wrote it down to send another print to her in Rome."

52

Back at the Hilton around 8:30 PM, Inbar didn't find Jonathan in their room. He descended to the concierge and asked about his son. The concierge said, "That strikingly handsome teenager. Who can miss him. He'd exited around eleven in the morning and hasn't come back yet."

Inbar sat in the lobby, waiting anxiously. Twenty minutes later Jonathan entered through a revolving door. Michael stood up and rapped, "Where have you been?"

"Relax," Jonathan laughed, dropping into a lobby chair. "You're like a Jewish mother. I'm fifteen already. I had an exciting day, but it wasn't a cloak and dagger sort of thing. You watch too many movies like 'Demons and Angels'. But this is the real world. Sit here and I'll tell you. It certainly wasn't a usual tourist day."

"You're going back home tomorrow, Jonathan," Inbar edicted after Jonathan finished his account. "I'm a panicky father indeed, you don't want to give me a heart attack. Right?"

*

And so it happened that on the next day Inbar dropped his son off at Fiumicino airport and drove from there directly to the address scribbled on the backside of a photo taken almost thirty years before.

53

A twenty something girl answered the doorbell this time.

"Can I talk to Carla Benvenuti?" Inbar asked, referring to the name scribbled on the photograph.

"Who's my grandmother to you, sir? I'm afraid she's over your age group. Though you're old enough yourself," came the reply.

Here goes again, he grumbled inwardly and repeated the story. The girl led him inside, called out in Italian and stood there. "I'll translate for you," she offered. "Good girl," he said, as a white haired strumpet walked in clutching an aluminum walker. *This is going to take some work,* he thought.

At the end, it took money where talking didn't work to get the story. A man had brought her a baby with instructions to take it to the Monastery in Assisi in the beginning of 1983, offering good money to her. She was also paid to visit the child occasionally to ensure they're taking good care of him. After some visits she became very attached to the toddler. "Affectionate even," the granddaughter translated, sounding bemused. But she stopped after a few months because she never got another payment. No, she doesn't remember the man who'd brought the baby. Nor what he looked like. That was over thirty years ago.

*

Back at Fiumicino a high school friend called "Michael!" and hugged Inbar. They passed the special security check for Tel Aviv bound flights and went into the plane where the guy split, saying "I also always fly first class, but this time my secretary booked me a coach seat. She's so dumb."

"Come sit with me then," Inbar offered. "Usually nobody flies first class on these three hour flights. Not everybody's bank account is inflated like mine, for all the wrong reasons." They went together to the front of the plane. The stewardess asked Inbar if he wants something to drink. He asked for coffee. His friend then asked for a glass of whiskey. She brought the drinks. Ten minutes into the flight he asked for a second and she brought him that. Fifteen minutes later he motioned to the stewardess with his index for another glass, "neither shaken nor stirred," he giggled. She sounded off, "Get back to your proper seat at economy, sir." He growled and stood up, followed by Inbar. The stewardess called after Inbar, "You're a legitimate first class passenger. I wasn't sending you to economy." He gabbed, "What difference does that make girl. I don't care where I sit for a few hours on a plane, one way or another."

54

In the beginning of summer Zalman Ganot paid Inbar a visit at the inspector's office. He just knocked on the door and walked in, greeting. Inbar grunted, "What brings you to my office, Zalman?"

"The curious matter of your daughter's friend. A little bird told me yesterday of some unusual results of a DNA test. I brought you something that could possibly serve as a basis for comparative analysis." He sat on the chair across from Inbar, putting a plastic envelope on the desk and adding, "If any DNA could be extracted from this ancient material."

"Where does this come from, Zalman?"

"Remember what I'd told you about the Talpiot ossuaries' bones? I skipped telling you that while working on one of the bone boxes, I took some biological matter from it. Now you have that on your desk."

"Just like you, Zalman. Which particular box does it come from?"

"The Tenth."

"I thought you had only nine,"

"There were ten ossuaries initially, but one later disappeared. That's the one I borrowed this stuff from."

164

Inbar took the plastic envelope, exited his office and handed it to his secretary, instructing her to send the material to the DNA forensic lab.

Five days later Inbar went to the lab at Mount Scopus, where a forensic officer informed him that they were able to extract mitochondrial DNA from his latest dispatch and compare it to the mitochondrial DNA taken from Josiah ben David's hair. "Results?" asked Inbar.

"The sequences are almost completely identical. Had they been contemporaries they would indicate maternal siblings."

"You mean they would have come from brothers?"

"To be precise Inspector, they would definitely have come from sons of the same mother."

55

At 09:31 on July 14 the computer of a NORAD technician in the Cheyenne Mountain Air Force Station (CMAFS) suddenly blipped "Missile Warning." The technician pushed an alert button. Another technician announced "Iranian missile warning." Seconds later an analyst delivered, "Estimated re-entry 17:34 Zulu and 17:49 Zulu."

The CMAFS commanding officer, a Brigadier General, entered the control hall and uttered "what targets?" The analyst closest to him relayed "2 IRBMs. Confirmed targets Tel Aviv in 4 minutes, Rome in 9 minutes."

An operative said to the commander, "The President and the Chairman of Joint Chiefs are informed."

"Go to DEFCON 3," the commander called out. Then he told the operative, "Get me the President on the phone."

*

At that precise moment in Jerusalem's Wailing Wall plaza hundreds of Jews were ritually lamenting the destruction of the Temple on the annual fast day of Tisha Be'av. Suddenly a young man appeared standing on top of the ancient wall facing them and proclaimed in a loud voice over the multitudes, "Behold, O Lord, and raise up their king, the son of David, at the time you have appointed, to reign over Israel your servant; and gird him with strength to crush unjust rulers; to cleanse Persia from the heathen that tread it underfoot, to cast out sinners from Your inheritance; to break the pride of enemies and all their strength as potter's vessels with a rod of iron; to destroy the evil nations with the words of his mouth; to gather his holy followers and lead them in righteousness. He shall glorify the Lord before all the earth and cleanse the Mullahs in holiness, as in the beginning. From the ends of the earth all nations shall come to see his glory and bring the weary sons of Zion as gifts; to see the glory of the Lord with which God has crowned him; for he is over them a righteous king taught of God. In his days there shall be no unrighteousness in their midst; for they are all holy and their king the anointed of the Lord."

"I'm watching everything from the Situation Room," the President said. "Is this really happening, General?"

"Affirmative Madam President. We're tracking two intermediate range Iranian missiles fired at Tel Aviv and Rome."

"Can we stop them?"

"No, we can't, since your predecessor scrapped that missile defense complex in Poland."

A CMAFS technician announced, "Thirty seconds to impact Tel Aviv."

"The Israelis should fire their Arrow ABMs now," the commander estimated.

Another technician called, "Two ABMs fired from Israel."

Tense silence followed for twenty three seconds. Then the technician cheered, "Tel Aviv IRBM killed."

The CMAFS technician announced, "Three minutes to impact Rome."

"Would the Italians shoot it down, General?" the President asked.

"They don't have Israel's ABM capabilities, Madam."

"Good lord," the President exclaimed. She then watched the situation screen in horrified shortage for another 90 seconds.

"10...9...8..." came the reading of the CMAFS announcer. A technician then hollered "Rome missile dead!"

On the next morning in her bedroom the President leafed through newspapers. All front pages were devoted entirely to the previous night's drama. Several reported a bizarre incident in Jerusalem concurrent with destruction of the Iranian missiles. Two related that many Orthodox Jews claim the young man who'd spoken from atop the Wailing Wall brought about the demise of Satan's assault.

The President powered her TV. The grave face of Ariel Sharon filled the screen addressing his nation in Hebrew simultaneously translated into English.

"...I reckoned from the beginning that the analogy between Iran's apologists in the West at this time and Nazis' apologists in the 30s was striking. Then and now, they naively believed that only the Jews have to worry. Then and now, the Russians shortsightedly first allied with evil. But of course these were just ruses by evil. In both cases evil regimes' ambitions went much farther than the Jews. Yesterday they attacked Rome, undoubtedly because of its great significance to Western civilization. And with theocratic Iran, the main target always was and is the United States of America.

Iran openly calls for the destruction of the United States and overtaking of the entire world by Islam. It pushes its Shi'a extremist, apocalyptic, jihadist ideology and its recently departed President invoked the 12th Imam before every speech, even at the U.N. Iran supports much terrorism in the world and installed terrorist puppet organizations in Lebanon and Gaza.

The West could virtually eliminate the Hitler imitators of this century but until the change of administration in Washington it did nothing effective to prevent Iran's suicidal, apocalyptic, jihadist regime from getting the Bomb. Realist Western leaders should have known that sanctions won't stop it. Only military action could. They should realize by now that as harsh as the consequences may have been, they'd be infinitely harsher later.

But what concerns me most and immediately as Israel's Prime Minister is Iran's unbound hatred for everything Jewish. It officially mocks and denies the holocaust and the existence of Israel and calls for genocide of the Jews of this country. Yesterday it tried to implement its evil plan against us. The Mullahs failed this time... I'm not going to give them a second try at wiping us off the map.

I believe that killing even millions of Iranians won't stop the Mullahs. Those who love individual suicide bombers would adore a collective suicide, even of their own people. This is why Mutual Assured Destruction that worked as effective deterrent of the pragmatic Soviets during the Cold War in the 20th century didn't work with theocratic Iran. But there's one thing that would stop them cold. Destruction of their Shi'a religious symbols. I believe threatening that is much preferable to attacking the theocracy's captive civil population.

I therefore formally issue the following ultimatum to Iran's leadership. Unless they totally capitulate, we would use their own medicine on their holiest Shi'a sites and destroy them one after another. We'd start a week from today by vaporizing one of these symbols. It's now up to the Mullahs to prevent that."

The phone rang on the President's night stand. She picked it up. "Good morning Madam President," the Secretary of State chimed in.

"I've heard that just now," she interjected. "Come over to the oval office at nine A.M."

*

At an air force base in Israel, Squadron Leader Wreckful standing before his pilots assembled in their combat briefing room cited Brigadier General Amir Eshel after he'd flown over Auschwitz-Birkenau,

> *"We pilots of the Israeli air force flying in the skies above the camp of horrors, arose from the ashes of the millions of victims and shoulder their silent cries, salute their courage and promise to be the shield of the Jewish people and the nation of Israel."*

58

"I had some difficulty getting here on time," the Secretary of State grumbled. "There's a demonstration going for the Israeli Embassy. I hear there are also demonstrations against Israel in most European capitals."

"What else is new," gestured the President. "European leftists' behavior is conditioned by cultural relativism, guilt complexes over past colonialism and old fashioned Jew hatred. Our Liberals are confounded by similar naïve notions, except that their minds are clouded with notions of 'US Imperialism' replacing Europeans' colonialism."

"If Sharon's threat materializes there'd be huge demonstrations in the Muslim world."

"Not in Sunni countries. They don't care about Shi'a shrines. Anyway, we won't get to that point."

"You think Sharon is bluffing?"

"No. He's a straight shooter. But he's read the Mullahs correctly. They'd go to the brink and blink first."

"I'm worried about a replay of the Hiroshima and Nagasaki scenario."

"I don't believe so. But if that happens, I couldn't blame Sharon. I'd have wiped Iran off the map already if they fired a nuclear missile at us. And I don't lead a nation that actually knows what genocide means."

"But Madam, since we're no longer subject to an immediate nuclear threat from Iran, I suggest we try to engage in some diplomacy with them. They'd be more forthcoming as they must have reevaluated their perceived military strength."

"That presupposes that theocratic Iran is a normal

state. The same mistake that the previous administration committed. My predecessor's perverse Iran policy stemmed from naïve detachment from Middle East strategic reality. We won't repeat that mistake."

*

The President proved correct. Six days later the Iranian government offered to give "immediate, unconditional and active cooperation" with U.N. and IAEA nuclear inspections. Despite wide international pressure on Israel to accept that, Sharon refused, demanding a capitulation of the Iranian army, Revolutionary Guard Units and militias; provisional occupation by NATO forces; search and destruction of any and all WMDs in Iran, including nuclear material and facilities; outlawing of the parties supporting the regime and democratic elections within a year. On the seventh day the Mullahs surrendered. The world outside of Iran sighed in relief. Days later huge demonstrations erupted in Iran and the regime was overthrown even before the actual implementation of the specific terms of capitulation had begun.

With the beginning of Autumn a current of messianic fervor was spreading through emotional contagion among many Jews and in large parts of Christendom. It was centered around a charismatic young man. Newspapers carried stories about him and his face graced the cover pages of international magazines. He called himself Josiah ben David and his message to his followers was, "Do Not Be Afraid." Jews claimed that he was the long-awaited Messiah, come at this time to help them cope with existential threats and to maintain Israel's redemption and revival at the climax of Jewish history. Reform and Liberal Jews were talking of a "messianic age" when Israel and The Nations will live in peace, harmony and Justice. But the Orthodox among Jews rejected the man because he wasn't a pious Jew and a Torah scholar. Christians believed he'd come to solve the enigma of a departed Messiah and inaugurate the Kingdom of Heaven after leading the faithful to final victory over the forces of darkness, as foretold in the Book of Revelations.

I remember this guy, the United States President thought, having read an interview with Josiah ben David in a leading national news magazine. He's the young orator who stood atop the Wailing Wall in Jerusalem dispensing biblical style hyperbole just before that Iranian nuclear missile broke up harmlessly over Rome. She instructed her secretary to set an appointment with the Director of the CIA. "Tell him I want to know everything we have on Salvatore de Luca aka Josiah ben David," she instructed. "I mean expansively, as long as it takes."

"The story begins with the finding in 1980 of an ancient family tomb in Jerusalem's East Talpiot neighborhood," recounted the CIA Director. "Is it superfluous to speak about that, Madam President?"

"I want you to tell me all expansively, there might be facts I don't know yet."

"The Israel Antiquities Authority (I.A.A.) came to the scene and kept the tomb controlled and the find documented, so we know that all findings there were authentic."

"As opposed to many artifacts in that country that have been found to be fake."

"Precisely, Madam. They are deemed suspect especially when their provenance is unknown. Not the subject case. "

"Continue please."

"Six ossuaries inscribed with names were found in the East Talpiot tomb, as follows:

1. 'Jesus son of Joseph;'

2. 'Joseph;'

3. 'Mary;'

4. 'Mary;'

5 'Matthew;'

6. 'Judah, son of Jesus.'

Four other ossuaries were said to have no name inscriptions. They were all taken to an I.A.A facility in Jerusalem for cleaning and further examination. One of these ossuaries somehow disappeared. Not before an I.A.A. official named Zalman Ganot hid a chunk of biological remains in his pocket.

The leader of the archeologists team believed that the tomb had belonged to Jesus' family. We don't know if he'd relayed his opinion to the Israeli government. In any event, a story went out that the ossuaries were empty when they were found. And that the bones of Joseph, Mary, Jesus son of Joseph, the other Mary and the rest of the family had already been vandalized, probably in antiquity. Later reports said the ossuaries did contain desiccated bones and other human remains.

The Vatican exerted much pressure on the Israelis to keep the matter confidential. A few days after the finding, the bones contained in the first ossuary were transferred to Italy. The other skeletons were reburied in accordance with Israeli law.

The matter remained unknown to the general public and even to most specialists and scholars in the world. In November 1995 a Jerusalem detective named Michael Inbar stumbled on it while conducting a routine burglary investigation. Then in April 1996 it got media attention from the London Sunday Times and B.B.C. In 2005/6 two books related, while another book was fully premised on it. In 2007 a TV documentary about it aired on the Discovery channel. That brought world-wide attention and heated debates on the question whether it is the real thing. Some experts and scholars opine it is, most profess the opposite view.

In 1983 in Rome a newborn baby was baptized and registered under the name 'Salvatore de Luca.' He grew up in the town of Assisi and was ordained as a priest. In 2006 he basically emigrated to Israel and changed his name to 'Josiah ben David.' His DNA examined in Israel establishes he's a pure Israelite, which is unique for a person living today. In addition, he's at least a maternal brother of the person whose bones Zalman Ganot had sneaked out of the missing tenth Talpiot ossuary. That's basically the story, Madam."

"Do you think what I'm thinking?" she whispered.

"I don't think, Madam. We know. Salvatore de Luca was cloned from the biological matter extracted from the ossuary that was inscribed 'Yeshua bar Yehosef', translating to 'Jesus son of Joseph.'"

"But of course it isn't Jesus Christ," The President exclaimed.

"Of course."

AUTHOR'S NOTE

The messianic proclamations of "Josiah ben David" in chapters 27, 43 and 55 above are based on ancient Dead Sea Scrolls texts, translated by Geza Vermes.

Thanks to my genial son Byron "Reckful" Bernstein for editing this book.

Encino, California December 4, 2011.